AIR BOAT

JACEK WALISZEWSKI

Publisher, Copyright, and Additional Information

Air Boat by Jacek Waliszewski

First edition, Copyright © 2022

KDP ISBN - 9798839286757

Edited by Jesse Winter at Duo Storytelling
Cover design and interior design by Rafael Andres

In memory of Pierce

1949–2020

Chapter 1

Flathead Lake is the largest body of water in Montana. It was carved out by a glacier's eonic scrape, then filled by thousands of years of glacial melt until it was more than three hundred feet deep. The trees along the lake's border are tall and only occasionally displaced by snowdrifts, forest fires, or a new cabin. The lake is twenty-five miles long, fifteen across, and contains several islands, the largest being Wild Horse, which some would say looks like a fish swimming east.

The mountains are closer to the water's edge along the eastern shore, and it is there that a blue pickup truck approaches the Yellow Bay State Park sign. The sun has just started to rise, and the truck drives with its headlights on while the exhaust puffs clear white haze.

Brothers Osborne's "Make it a Good One" plays from one of the open windows, and the truck slows before turning off Highway 35. It moves onto a gravel road, approaches the boat launch, and parks to the side.

Luke is in his early thirties, well built, and has a scruffy two-week beard. He adjusts the well-worn Glacier National Park baseball hat on his head, turns off the engine, and shuts the door. He walks to the back of the truck and drops the tailgate. He pulls a kayak out and drags it to the water. The sleeves on his Henley shirt are bunched up, and he straightens them out, then secures his rod, bait box, and thermos in the kayak.

He paddles south of the Flathead Lake Biological Station peninsula. The finger of land looks like a small version of Florida, and a flock of thirty Canadian geese, who have never been to Miami, float where the panhandle would have been. They eye Luke, this early morning intruder, but deem his steaming thermos of coffee and quiet presence not to be a threat.

Luke casts his line.

There is a small silent splash.

The morning is otherwise still and only punctuated by a goose's sleepy *gonk*, recast, or jump of a fish in the distance. But time yields to eventuality, and the day gives way to the rest of the world.

Luke turns his ear at the sound of a distant motorboat. It is a soft rumble, thick and throaty. It is steadily coming toward him but blocked from sight by the peninsula. The geese hear it too and start to pop their heads up. They, like Luke, are frustrated at the wake the boat is about to bring.

But there is no boat.

The sun glints off the silver wings of an airplane as it flies low and under the tree line. It is only a few feet above the lake, and the plane's body is thick in the front and angled at the rear. Two sturdy pontoons hang under the winglets, and the red tail is complemented by a black stallion decal. The Grumman Widgeon is from World War II and was designed to patrol coastal waters, but it is now here in Montana, nearly seven hundred miles from the nearest ocean.

Luke admires the plane for its mechanical beauty, but the Canadian geese do not. They sound the alarm at this metal pterodactyl, flap their wings, and spread frantic lines of whitewash. The flock rises with slow inevitability, and it is apparent to Luke and the pilot that the geese will fly directly in front of the plane's flight path. The pilot turns slightly and dips low to avoid the birds. The plane's nose glances the water and passes safely under the birds. But it is now flying directly at Luke at more than a hundred miles an hour.

Luke's eyes grow wide in realization, and he flips himself out of the kayak. He swims hard down toward the rocks and turns to look above him. The underside of the plane's bow churns toward him, the engine's reverberations grow, and the winglet buoys skim a wake of their own. The plane approaches his kayak and lifts to spare it by no less than a foot. Then, as quickly as it arrived, the plane is gone.

Luke punches out of the water and takes a deep breath. The adrenaline prevents him from feeling the cold, but he knows it will happen soon since the lake is fed year-round by snowmelt. He hangs on to the kayak and catches sight of the plane. It makes a long arc around the southern portion of Yellow Bay and comes back at a higher altitude.

The pilot can barely be seen behind a large pair of aviator glasses.

Luke is a small speck in the water and curses at the plane with a raised fist.

But the pilot can't hear or help him, and after seeing he is okay, the plane waves its wings in an apology, then flies away.

With nothing else to resolve, Luke flips his kayak right side up. His bait box floats with half the contents spilled, and after a more committed search, he can't find his fishing rod.

He rightfully assumes it has sunk.

"Dammit!" he splashes.

* * *

Luke pulls his kayak up the boat ramp. Water squirts out of his boots as he slides it into the back of his truck. He purses his lips and unlocks the door, sees his seat, and wonders how long his boots will take to dry. He takes his shirt off after a moment of deliberation, rings the water out, and drives away.

* * *

The sun is only slightly higher by the time Luke pulls up to a bait and tackle store. The bungalow building is next to the water. One wall is dedicated to all things boating—bait, tackle, and life vests. On the other wall, a garage-sized cooler is full of cases of light beer, and a red-checkered short-order kitchen is in the back of the building. A vintage board advertises burgers, fries, and milkshakes.

Luke parks and sees the infamous red-tailed plane tied to the dock.

He gets out of his truck with a stern look on his face, and Katie, the old cashier, sees him storm in.

"Hi, Luke," she says.

Luke nods to Katie, then looks through the windows at the plane. A tall middle-aged man with a sweater vest and jeans stands on the dock. The old man is inspecting the propellers and says something to a young woman in her midtwenties. She is wearing a T-shirt and ball cap and is pumping gas into the plane's fuel tank.

"Katie. Can you tell me who owns that plane? And good morning," Luke corrects, remembering his manners.

The two of them look outside. The young woman puts the fuel nozzle away and points at the numbers on the gas pump. The man shakes her hand and starts walking back to the shop.

Katie looks down at a clipboard. "Murphy. Forty gallons."

Luke walks closer to the back window and studies the man. He looks plump, well dressed, and in no rush.

"Murphy, huh?"

"Ah, yup. Hey, you okay?" Katie asks, sensing Luke's frustrated energy.

"Yeah, I'm fine, I just got to have a little talk with Mr. Murphy."

Katie is about to say something when the brass bell on the back door dings and Mr. Murphy comes in.

"Murphy! You son of a bitch!" Luke starts.

The old man is caught off guard. "What?" he asks, looking behind him.

Luke is not in any mood for theatrics. "You nearly killed me out there!"

Murphy stutters. "How?"

"You ran me over!" Luke points to the lake.

The man looks past Luke toward the parking lot. "I did? When?"

"Yeah!"

There's an awkward pause, and Murphy thinks for a moment. "But I haven't driven since yesterday."

"Driven?" Luke asks. "You were flying, today, at Yellow Bay."

Murphy recognizes Luke's confusion and is confident he isn't responsible for whatever irked him so. "Son, I'm renting that cabin," he says, indicating one up on the hill. He then walks past Luke to the store's self-serve counter and pours himself a cup of coffee. "I just got out of bed half an hour ago, and perhaps more importantly, my name *isn't* Murphy."

Luke turns back to Katie. "I thought you said his name *was* Murphy?"

Katie shakes her head and suppresses a grin. "No, I said *Murphy* bought gas. *That's* Murphy," she clarifies, pointing at the plane.

The woman with the T-shirt sits in the cockpit of the plane and puts on her sunglasses. She pushes a lever, turns a knob, and starts one of the engines. The propeller turns, and she throttles it with confidence. She backs the plane away from the dock and starts the second engine. When they are synchronized, the flaps are tested, and the plane moves through the marina like any other boat. Once it is clear of the last buoy, the engines throttle up in full, and the hull starts to rise the faster it goes along the lake. Water sprays in wide sheets, the plane skims the surface like a skipping stone, and it rises into the air a few seconds later.

Katie grins, then nods at the wall of gear. "So, you need a new fishing rod?"

Luke shakes his head and turns to the older man. "And to apologize. Sorry."

Not-Murphy takes a sip of his coffee. "Sounds complicated."

Chapter 2

Tucked behind a mountain ridge, Luke stands on the sharply angled roof of a one-story cabin. It is squat, with a slightly leaning brick chimney, and is wrapped by a wide covered porch. The high peaks of the Swan Range dominate the view, and a small clearing spreads out in front of the home. Luke wears a sturdy leather tool belt and has pried several wooden shingles off the roof.

He tosses the bad ones to the side and hammers new ones in their place.

When he stands to wipe the sweat from his brow, something near his truck catches his eye. A husky sits calmly near the front wheel. The gray and white dog has been watching him for more than a minute, and Luke sees that it only has three legs.

He is intrigued and takes the ladder to the ground. He approaches the dog and extends the back of his hand. The dog sniffs him and wags his tail, and Luke scratches him behind his ear.

"Hello," he says.

The dog looks around.

"Are you lost?"

The dog yawns, and Luke sees the collar around its neck. He rotates it to the tag, which only has a name.

Saint.

"Well, Saint. How are you?"

Saint barks, and Luke kneels to further check him out. He spends a moment looking at the stump of his missing leg, which healed long ago.

"Where'd you come from? And how'd you get here on only three legs?"

Saint walks over to the truck and pees on the tire.

Luke laughs. "Well, all right. I was about to have lunch. Want some?"

Saint looks at him and cocks an ear.

Luke walks into the cabin and, after some kitchen activities, exits with a bowl of water and two ham sandwiches. He puts the water on the stairs, then places a sandwich next to it before stepping away to sit in an old rocking chair.

"Yours if you want it."

Saint looks at him, then the bowl and food. He moves slowly to the stairs, sniffs the water, and eats the sandwich in two bites. He licks his mouth and is distracted by something in the woods.

Two deer walk along the wood line. They make no noise, but they have been seen. Saint's ears perk, and after an evaluative pause, the dog gives chase. The deer run nimbly through the woods, and Saint chases after them like a trampling beast.

Luke waves a goodbye. "Good luck, buddy."

* * *

Later, at a hardware store in Kalispell, Luke pushes a flatbed cart through the lumber aisle. Another hardware cart pusher, Crail, comes around the corner. He is balding and in his midfifties, and he has a very comfortable beard and belly. He carries a shopping list and squints at it—he doesn't want to get eyeglasses despite having all the reasons to do so.

Luke sees him first. "Crail, buddy, what's going on?"

Crail looks up. "Luke, long time no see. How's the cabin?"

Luke lifts a few wooden boards from his cart. "You think these will make for good trim pieces?"

Crail shrugs. "Sure. Need me to bring anything over? Nail gun?"

"No, thanks, I think I have it under control. Just taking longer than I thought." Luke then looks over into Crail's cart. It has multiple axes and a bag of birdseed. "How's the axe throwing business?"

Crail beams. "Better than ever. Oh! Speaking of, we're doing a thirty-year anniversary tomorrow night. Sally would be more than happy if you swung by. It won't be all that exciting for a young guy like you — us old-timers will probably just end up playing poker. You play?"

Luke grins. "I'll play so long as you don't complain if I take your money."

Crail smiles. "Great! Got a date?"

Luke shakes his head. "No. Just me. What should I bring?"

"I don't know. What does anyone bring to an anniversary? A pie or something?"

Luke chuckles. "A pie or something it will be."

* * *

The next night, Luke drives down a two-lane, yellow-striped road. A boxed huckleberry pie is on the passenger seat, and Luke listens to country music. He lightly taps the steering wheel while paying close attention to the turns in front of him. The headlights illuminate just past the next crest, and he drives a few miles an hour slower than recommended just in case a bear or moose makes its evening crossing. Expecting this, Luke sees a flash of white fur and immediately takes his foot off the gas. He slows and sees Saint trotting confidently down the road.

Luke slows even more and rolls down the passenger window. "Saint!"

Saint stops and looks at him, and Luke turns on his blinker and pulls over. He gets out and walks around. "I don't normally pick people up from the side of the road," Luke starts. "But you're not exactly people, are you? Need a ride?"

Saint's ears tilt and he looks in both directions.

"I'm going to a dinner party and need a wingman," Luke adds.

Saint grumble-barks, and Luke opens the passenger door. Saint sniffs the seat, then tries to jump in but slips on account of his missing leg.

Luke feels foolish.

"Ah, let me help." He lifts Saint in, shuts the door, and walks back to the driver's side. By the time he gets in, Saint has eaten half the pie.

Luke evaluates the situation. "Well… at least it wasn't wasted."

He checks the rearview mirror, flicks the blinker, and heads back down the road.

* * *

They pull up to a large modern home on the outskirts of Kalispell a while later. Several cars line the street, and the large bay windows show multiple people inside. Luke parks in the driveway and leaves Saint inside the truck. He walks up the stairs and knocks.

Sally, who is in the prime of her fifties, opens the door. She immediately smiles and takes Luke in for a hug.

"So glad you could make it."

"I had a pie," he confesses. "But my date ate it."

"Date? Where is she?" she asks excitedly.

"He," Luke corrects.

Sally is caught off guard. "Oh. Well… he must have been hungry. Is he coming?"

Luke points at the truck. "Well, he's a dog, but I'd like to know if it's okay for him to come in."

Sally starts laughing and playfully smacks Luke on the arm. "Luke, oh my. Okay, well, is he at least potty trained?"

"I don't really know. He came around my place, and I just saw him on the side of the road. He's got a collar, so he's someone's dog. Probably just lost."

Sally thinks for a moment. "Well, if he's got your vote of approval, then he's good enough for me. Go get your *date* and come inside. You know, though" — she laughs — "next party, you may want to consider someone… more *human.*"

Luke grins, his dimples showing, and he starts back to the truck. "I've tried that," he says over his shoulder. "But it just never seems to work out."

She waits for him while he goes and opens the passenger door.

"Let's go, buddy. You've been formally requested," he says.

Saint comes to the edge of the seat and looks down. A whimper reminds Luke to help him out, and Saint walks by his side as they go to the house.

A banner reading "Married 30 Years!" drapes over the main living room, and multitudes of people with drink glasses and finger foods walk around in good spirits. Luke enters with Saint and Sally, and the kids in the house are drawn to them.

"Doggy!" several young voices yell.

The kids rush the door, and Luke instinctively steps in front of Saint.

"Stop!" he says firmly.

The kids stop, and Saint sits down.

Luke looks at Saint.

You're trained?

A kid missing his two front teeth is the first to speak. "Can we pet your dog?"

Luke looks at the kid. "Hand out like this." He shows how. "Let them smell you first. Then scratch the side of their ear, not over the head. And never put your face in front of theirs."

A kid with a bad haircut is confused. "Why?"

Luke grows somber. "Because. Might bite your face off."

"No way!" a few kids exclaim.

Luke kneels and shows them an old scar on his arm. "Yup. Big dog got me once when I was your age. Almost ate my whole arm."

Sally rolls her eyes and suppresses a laugh, and the kids look at Saint with renewed suspicion. They are concerned, and none of them move until Saint comes over and licks Luke's face.

He grins. "But Saint is a good dog. He just wants love."

"Where's his leg?" an inquisitive kid wonders aloud.

"Bear took it."

The kids shake their heads. "Nuh-uh!"

Luke nods. "Honest truth. Just ask Mrs. Sally."

Sally laughs. "You're not getting me involved in this."

"Can we pet him already?" the missing-toothed kid asks.

Luke gets up and puts his hands on his hips. "All right… but show me how."

The kids all stand in front of Saint. They present their hands one by one, and Saint smells them individually. He is scratched behind the ear in return.

Sally looks at Luke. "Are you satisfied?"

"Yes."

Crail comes out of the kitchen. He has a burger in one hand and a beer in the other. "Luke! You made it. And a dog?"

Sally puts a hand on Crail's shoulder. "It's fine."

Crail nods and turns to Luke. "I've been informed that it's fine."

Luke laughs. "Yeah, thanks. Oh, Sally," he says. "Congratulations on thirty years. Crail's all the better for it, but I'm not sure what you got out of it."

"Oh, I think I did pretty good," she counters, taking Crail by the arm.

"Yes, yes you did," Crail confirms. He then turns to Luke. "Poker?"

Luke looks down at Saint. He is on his back and receiving multiple belly rubs. Sally pushes Luke and Crail away. "He'll be fine," she says. "I'll make sure of it. You two, now get."

They move through the kitchen to the garage. Saint sees Luke leaving and follows. Luke stops by the table, which is full of food, and puts a burger on a bun. Saint sits down next to him and murmurs in anticipation.

Luke tosses two patties to Saint, who eats them quickly.

In the garage, the poker table is round and circled by guys of various ages. The garage door is partially open, one man smokes a cigar, and another wears a visor. Luke walks in, and he and Crail take two open seats.

Saint lies down under Luke's chair.

The cards are dealt, but the men do not talk to each other. They interact as if they were old trees who would only talk when there was something of particular importance to share.

"So, Luke here is building a cabin," Crail says halfway through the first hand.

No one says anything, but chips are put in.

Luke shakes his head, then checks his cards. "Remodeling, not quite building."

There are several checks and raises.

Green-Visor humphs to himself. "Lots of people do that," he says with a hint of museful disdain. He then takes the better part of a minute to decide what to do with his cards before starting up again. "All romantic about it when they start, never finish when they realize it's real work."

"Or the winters drive them out," Cigar-Smoker adds quietly.

There's a moment of consideration, cards are shown, and Cigar-Smoker wins.

Everyone is dealt another hand.

"Luke knows real work," Crail says. "Don't worry about that."

Green-Visor looks over at Luke, then his own cards. "What'd you do before wanderlusting to Montana?"

Luke puts some chips out. "That was a different life."

Crail fills in the gap. "Army."

Cigar-Smoker nods. "Thank you for your service. I was a marine."

Luke grins. "Then thank you for *your* service. You had the harder job."

They both chuckle and plays a few chips.

"What did you do in the army?"

"Army stuff," Luke deflects.

Marine nods. He's respectfully aware of Luke's lack of desire to answer and looks down at Saint. "Good dog. Well trained."

Luke nods and reaches down. "Found him wandering around. Has a collar, but it just has his name."

Green-Visor looks at Saint. "You checked his microchip?"

"No. Not yet." Luke says simply. "Tomorrow maybe."

Green-Visor chuckles to himself. "My sister had a dog. The microchip in its scruff kept disappearing, so she got it rechipped the next year. Year after that, *that* chip went missing. After that, she went every year to get it rechipped. Turns out the little RFID capsule was just slipping down over into the dog's shoulder. The damn dog had four microchips before they figured it out." Green-Visor laughs and shakes his head. "When I asked her why she didn't ask the vet what was happening, she said she thought the subscription was for keeping the chip turned *on*, not the online *registration*."

A collection of laughs and snickers erupts, and the old trees have bonded.

* * *

Luke pulls up to a local veterinarian the next morning. Saint sits in the front seat, and they exchange a look.

"Well, we've got to go," Luke says to him.

He takes a length of rope and ties it to Saint's collar. He opens the truck door, picks Saint up, and puts him on the sidewalk. They enter the quaint office. Pictures of dogs and cats line the hall, and a large silver animal scale sits in the corner.

Marsha, the secretary, is at a desk.

"Good morning!" she welcomes with genuine friendliness. "How are we today?"

Luke rubs the back of his neck. "Hi, I, uh, found a dog. Do you scan chips?"

"Sure, let's check."

She picks up a telephone-sized wand and comes around the desk. She pets Saint, puts the scanner to his scruff, and rubs it around. It beeps and displays a number.

"Now we just need to reference it."

She goes back to the desk and types in a few numbers.

"And that's that! Minnesota."

"What? He came all the way over here?" Luke asks.

Marsha shrugs. "Huskies love to roam, and this one looks to have a hint of wolf in him. But that sure is a long way to travel." She writes the number on a sticky note, then hands it to Luke. "Here's the phone number on record."

Luke looks at the note. "Thanks. How much do I owe you?"

"Oh, stop it. That didn't take anything."

* * *

Back in the truck, Luke looks at the sticky note while Saint pants. A squirrel is in a tree and has captured Saint's full attention.

Luke forces himself to call the number.

A gruff voice answers.

"Hello?"

"Hi, I'm Luke. I think I found your dog."

"The husky?"

"Yes. Saint."

"Hmm… Saint. He isn't my dog. I've never had a dog. That animal runs away often enough. I get called two or three times a year about him."

Luke looks at the number. "But this is your number?"

"Yup. This is my number. They must have put it in the database wrong."

"Are you from Minnesota?"

"Yes. Where's the dog gone off to now?"

"Montana."

Gruff Voice is surprised. "Montana? That's the furthest yet. Once I got a call from Canada, but that's just across the way."

Luke looks over at Saint, who is watching the squirrel run across a telephone line.

"So, no one knows who he belongs to?" Luke asks to clarify.

There's a sigh on the other line. "How long you had him?"

"Just a day."

"Well, if he hasn't run off, I'd assume he's yours till he does."

Luke rubs behind Saint's ear. He sees a pet store in his rearview mirror and considers the advice. "Guess he just might be."

* * *

The truck pulls up to the cabin. Luke gets out, and Saint comes to the driver's side and lets himself be brought down to the ground. Luke pulls a few things out of the back of the truck bed—dog food, silver bowls, a leash, a dog bed. He heaves the food bag over a shoulder and carries it into the cabin. Saint walks around and smells the cabin corners, then watches Luke put the bowls and dog bed next to the rocking chair.

Luke fills the food bowl up and points at it. "This is yours."

He then goes inside the cabin to fill the water bowl.

Saint follows.

The interior is a simple, open, one-room concept with a fireplace, bed, and kitchen. A work in progress in every sense, the bathroom is the only room with a door on it.

Luke opens the vintage enameled fridge and pulls out some bread and deli meat. Smelling the ingredients, Saint sits patiently.

Luke shakes his head, then leads Saint outside to the dog bowl.

"Eat," he reiterates.

Saint has no reaction.

Luke takes a more commanding tone. "Good boy. Eat *your* food."

Saint's ears twitch but nothing else.

"What's the command for food? Good food? Eat away? Chow down?"

Saint stares at Luke, then passes a subtle glance at his sandwich. Luke sees this, then moves the sandwich from one hand to the other.

Saint stares at the sandwich as if it were another squirrel.

"Oh, you want *my* food?"

Saint mumbles in the affirmative.

Luke takes a demonstrative bite out of his sandwich. "This is not yours."

Saint lets out a quiet bark.

"No. I'm serious."

Saint grumbles.

Luke takes another bite, and Saint barks loudly.

"No! You're a dog. You eat *dog* food. I'm a human. I eat *human* food."

Saint gets up and goes to his dog bowl. He nudges it over, and dry food spills out. He then looks up at Luke expectantly.

"Oh, well now you've done it."

They stare at each other as the sky turns dark, and Luke considers his options.

He finally shakes his head and tosses his sandwich to Saint.

* * *

The sun rises, and Luke pushes his kayak out into the water at Yellow Bay. The geese started their journey south to Mexico a day earlier, and Saint paces and whines on the beach. He barks his disapproval the farther Luke gets, which, by the time he casts his first line, turns into an all-out bemoaning howl.

"I'm right here!" Luke exclaims.

Saint is having none of it and responds with a sad howl.

"Just let me catch three fish. Okay? Just three?"

Saint vocalizes the injustice of their separation, and Luke turns his kayak so he doesn't have to face it. He casts again, and Saint eventually quiets down. Luke nods to himself in satisfaction for having established his boundaries, but then Saint swims up to the kayak and struggles to get in.

"Dammit!" Luke says as the kayak starts to tip. He secures the rod and grabs Saint by the collar, then pulls him in and puts him on his lap. The kayak is unstable and dangerously close to taking on water, but Saint is satisfied. He pants and is comfortable in the small boat.

"Really?" Luke asks, leaning back to make room.

Saint licks his face but says nothing else.

* * *

Later that same day, they pull back up to the bay. Luke pulls out a large canoe from the back of his truck and puts it in the water.

Out in the bay, Saint sits stoically in the front while Luke paddles and casts.

There are no more disagreements.

Chapter 3

Luke carries football-sized river rocks from the bed of his truck into the cabin. Saint is lying inside next to the fireplace and watches Luke slather mortar on the rocks before fitting them against the exposed brick.

"You know," Luke says to Saint. "I could have ripped everything out and started clean, but the more material we have that can hold heat, the warmer we'll stay."

Saint looks at him, then over at the refrigerator.

Luke catches this glance. "You're not here to learn about the fireplace, are you?"

Saint's gaze stays locked on the fridge, and Luke points a finger at him.

"I knew it."

* * *

The sky streaks shades of orange and purple while wisps of smoke rise from the cabin's chimney. Luke sits in his rocking chair on the front deck with a camping plate on his lap. He cuts through a steak and savors each bite. While he chews, he wonders when he should start chopping wood and how much would be enough.

Saint, meanwhile, sleeps in his dog bed. There is a camping plate in front of him as well, but he ate his steak before Luke even had a chance to settle in his chair.

Saint's ears perk up, and his eyes open. He looks out but doesn't move his head. Luke sees this and wonders if it is another pair of deer, then notices a vehicle moving through the woods along his driveway.

Crail pulls up next to Luke's truck a short moment later.

"Luke! How you been?" he asks, getting out of his car. "Cabin is looking great."

Luke meets Crail at the top of the porch. "Yeah, thanks. Slowly but surely."

Saint gets in between them and demands attention. Crail gives him some while looking around.

"What's up? Everything okay?" Luke asks.

"Tried calling, no answer."

"No reception. I rather like it that way."

Crail nods. "Figured." He then sees the steak on Luke's rocking chair. "Got any more?"

Luke looks at Saint. "I did, till he wanted some. Cried me deaf till I got him fed. All I'm good for now is a sandwich or beer."

"Well, the dog is what I wanted to talk to you about."

"How so?"

Crail pulls a folded sheet of paper out of his back pocket and hands it to Luke. It's a "Missing Dog" poster, and Saint's name and picture are on the front.

SAINT, HUSKY, THREE LEGS, REWARD!

Luke considers the paper. "Well, damn."

Crail nods. "Yeah, sorry buddy."

"Can I just act like you didn't give me this?"

"Do whatever you want, but knowing you, that's probably not what you're going to do."

Luke sighs, looks back at the paper, then at Saint. "Well, can I at least wait till tomorrow?"

Crail raises his hands warmly, indicating he's not going to get involved. "You said something about beer?"

Luke runs his hand through his hair. "And a sandwich."

"Okay, but just one of each. Sally has been telling me to cut down."

Luke laughs and raises his hands, indicating he is also not going to get involved. "You do what you have to, man."

Crail chuckles and they walk into the cabin.

The fireplace is lit, and most of the mantle is resurfaced with rock. A few lightbulbs are on, and a radio plays in the corner.

"I like what you did with the fireplace."

Luke gets two beers and hands one over.

"Doing," he corrects. "But thanks. Taking longer than I thought, but no rush."

Crail looks up at the roofline. "Did you check the flue before lighting it?"

"For what?"

"Birds and squirrels like to make nests in the chimneys if they haven't been used for a while. Sometimes they catch fire."

Luke cracks the beer open and taps it to Crail's. "I did not, but I've run the fire for a few days now, might have just gotten lucky."

"Probably an old wives' tale. But hey, I'm serious, you can always stay with us if you don't get the place finished by winter. We've got a downstairs apartment and all. No shame."

"Too stubborn for that."

Crail takes a sip. "I've seen it snow ten feet in one night."

"I doubt that."

"Okay, maybe two or three. But still, if I have to get out here on a snowmobile to check on you, I'm taking you back with me."

Luke laughs. "Fair enough. If I'm ever being dumb, our safe word is now going to be *snowmobile*."

Crail thinks to himself. "I haven't had to use a safe word in years."

Luke spits out his beer. "I learn something new about you every time."

Crail shrugs, then helps himself to the fridge. He makes a sandwich, and they go out front. He and Luke lean on the rail and look out over the meadow. Several deer move along the field.

Crail points them out. "Hey, look over there," he says in a whisper.

Saint perks his head and sees them too. He murmurs and starts to shuffle.

Luke puts his hand down and snaps his fingers with simple authority. "No. Stay. Leave them be."

Saint lies back down but continues to grumble.

"So, forgot to tell you, almost got run over the other day," Luke tells Crail.

"What? How?"

"I was fishing. An air boat almost clipped me."

Crail is confused. "You mean a flatwater boat? From Florida?"

"No, no, the ones that fly. With pontoons."

"I, uh, think they're called seaplanes."

Luke shakes his head. "But we're on a lake, not the sea."

Crail shrugs. "Other than the name, what happened?"

"Dove in the water. Flipped my kayak. Lost my favorite rod."

Crail laughs and shakes his head. "Could only happen to you."

They say nothing else, and by the time Crail leaves, the deer have found somewhere safe to sleep, and the wisps of chimney smoke are only visible through the moon's rising light.

* * *

The next morning, the chimney is cold, and there is frost on the grass. A sheer line of sunshine melts the white crystals, leaving the ones in the shadows to wait their turn.

Luke steps out of the cabin with a cup of coffee.

He is barefoot and only wearing jeans, and his arms and chest tingle with goosebumps. He feels the chilly air but remains standing as if stubbornly undeterred. He notices a thin sheen of ice on his windshield, and the presence of snowy mountain caps in the distance. It isn't until a shiver runs up his back that he can no longer defy the inevitable.

Saint steps out of the cabin and stretches with a groan, his breath also visible.

"Want to do one walk around before we take you home?"

Saint finishes stretching, and Luke puts on boots and a sweater. They step off the porch and walk slowly down the driveway. Saint smells bushes and stumps along the way, and Luke can't shake the feeling of sadness. He ignores the heaviness within as they walk down the drive. The remnants of an old fence post marks the end of his property, and they turn along the forest line. They soon pass the spot where they had seen the deer, and Saint can't help but smell every tree in the immediate vicinity.

At the far end of the meadow, an old trail emerges. The listing agent told Luke it had once been the primary way to the property, but the county planners had established the main road further back, and his driveway connected to it. This trail, with its wagon wheel ruts no longer serving a purpose, was eventually reclaimed by the forest.

"Want to go up that way?" Luke asks, indicating what is left of the trail.

Saint stops and his hackles raise.

"What do you see? Another deer?"

Saint starts to growl and moves in front of Luke. Luke doesn't see anything and is about to walk past when a large brown bear, the size of a car, meanders onto the trail. Its nose smells the air, and its square-headed body turns to face the two. Sensing competition—or its next meal—it stands on its back legs to evaluate the situation.

Luke picks up a chunky branch and throws it at the bear. The branch crumbles midair in dry rot and doesn't hit, but the act of defiance is enough to make the bear angry.

It drops on all fours and roars.

Luke takes off his sweater and waves it in an attempt to make himself look bigger. "Hiya, bear! Get out of here!"

Saint, however, *has* grown bigger, and his teeth bare to show the wolf within him. He barks voraciously and bounds forward a few feet. His teeth snap like clapping boards, and spittle sprays with each successive show of force.

The bear, sensing too much to fight, drops back to the ground, turns, and lumbers back up the trail.

Saint is about to lunge after the bear, but Luke grabs his collar and holds him back. Saint snarls and barks regardless, refusing to give ground.

Luke commits to pulling him out to the field. "Get. Back. Here," he struggles.

Once safe in the open, he lets go of him, and Saint returns to being a dog. His hackles are smooth, and he pants with earned tiredness.

"I don't know what you were going to do there with just three legs, but, yeah, good looking out."

Saint licks Luke on the face and wags his tail but keeps a wary eye on the trail.

* * *

The sun is high in the blue sky when Luke and Saint drive into town. Luke checks his phone, and when he has reception, he calls the number on the lost-and-found poster. He speaks to an older-sounding man, Pierce, who is happy to know Saint has been found. Pierce gives him an address for a place on the west side of the lake.

Further into civilization, they stop at an intersection in Kalispell. Luke sees a lumber store, checks the time, and looks over at Saint.

"You know, maybe he meant *after* noon, not afternoon. Besides, they have good prices here, right?"

Saint says nothing.

Luke takes his silence as tacit agreement, and he pulls the truck into the hardware store parking lot. Saint follows him into the store on a leash, and Luke pushes the flatbed cart down the aisles. He slowly loads it with a few two-by-fours, some plywood, and a box of screws. He checks out the kitchen design area, and when he finds himself looking at garage door openers, he looks down at Saint and shakes his head.

"Yeah, I know."

Outside, Luke secures the beams in the bed of the truck. The wood sticks out of the bed by a foot and has no chance of falling out. Despite this, he takes the time to ask an attendant for a red flag. He uses twine to tie it onto the end of a two-by-four, then looks at the back of the cab. Saint watches Luke with round eyes, and Luke sighs. He knows he is just stalling, and with deep melancholy, walks to the other side of the truck. He gets in, rubs Saint's head, and pulls through the lot.

He is about to exit when he sees a food truck, and a few minutes later, Luke and Saint sit on a bench and eat hot dogs. After they are done, Saint settles down on the grass and takes a nap.

Luke looks around. Geese fly south in a V formation, and he checks his watch.

"I'm just delaying the inevitable," he says quietly.

* * *

The trees cast long shadows by the time Luke finds Pierce's address. He turns onto a smooth driveway and approaches a sprawling rustic home. Large carriage lights line the deeply forested way, and a long pier extends out onto the lake.

Luke whistles to himself. "Nice house, buddy. Why'd you run away?"

He parks in the roundabout, lifts Saint out, and knocks on the large wooden front door. An older man with streaks of gray hair and a button-down shirt opens it. He holds a glass of whiskey, and the deep crow's feet at the corners of his eyes compliment his smile.

He warmly presents his hand. "Luke, I presume? I'm Pierce."

"Pierce, nice to meet you," Luke says as they shake hands.

Saint pushes between them and enters the house. He grabs a dog toy and starts tossing it around as if he hadn't been gone at all.

Pierce and Luke watch.

"Thanks for bringing him back," Pierce says. "He gets away every once in a while."

"Likes to wander."

"That he does. Oh, Stella said there was a reward. Do you remember how much?"

Luke waves his hand. "Oh no, Saint is a good dog. I'm just glad he's home."

"Oh. Well…" Pierce ponders, then notices the glass in his hand, "Stella and her mom should be home soon. They were getting food for dinner. If you've got nothing going on, dinner is the least we can do."

Luke watches Saint play with the toy a while longer, then glances back at his truck. "I had intended on getting some remodeling done."

Pierce opens the door further. "Well, I'm not the one cooking, so you know it's going to be good."

Luke chuckles. "All right, I accept."

He enters the house and Pierce shuts the door. A fire roars in the fireplace, flanked by thick, plush couches, and Pierce goes to the bar.

"Bourbon or whiskey?"

"To be honest, I don't know the difference."

Pierce looks at the bottles. "Now that you mention it, neither do I."

Luke makes his way to the fireplace and inspects the mantle. It is solid wood. The grain's veins look as if they were lacquered a hundred years ago.

"This is beautiful."

"Thanks. This place has been in the family for generations, two hundred–plus years or so. Every generation added, never took away. Great-Great-Granddad Pierre was a French fur trader." He looks around and motions. "It used to be much smaller. Just the little footprint you're standing in."

Luke looks at the rows of pictures on the mantle. They span the ages. There is a young man in a crop duster, one of a few people floating on innertubes, then several other generational pictures. The photos culminate in a black-and-white portrait of a man with a large beard. He wears a patchwork of stitched-together furs and is presumably the one and only Great-Great-Grandfather Pierre.

"What did you add?" Luke asks.

"Perfect is the enemy of good!" Pierce jokes as he walks over and offers a drink. "My legacy is *maintain and keep it going*."

Luke points at the pictures. "Which one is you?"

Pierce taps a photo on the back row. It is of a young guy in uniform. "This here. I used to fly in the navy. Reconnaissance and all that. And that's Stella. Then there's my wife, Barbara. Prefers to be called Bee. Then the family throughout."

"Now what do you do?"

"Retired. Started a small air charter business."

"Jets?"

Pierce laughs. "No, nothing that fancy. The novel vintage vacation option. I fly clients from the West Coast—LA and Seattle mainly—then take them out to Alaska, Canada, and even here, Montana." He takes a sip, "What about you? What do you do?"

"Remodeling a cabin. About *this* big," he says, indicating half of the living room. "I used to be in the army. Medically retired."

Pierce sighs and remembers the three times he almost crash-landed due to one reason or another. "Yeah, military life will do that to you."

* * *

Pierce and Luke sit on Adirondack chairs on the deck. The sun is setting to their backs, and the lake is darkening. Saint lies between the two of them, and Pierce has half a cigar in one hand. They've sat for quite some time in silence, neither feeling the need to talk when the views were transitioning on such a majestic scale.

Something catches Saint's attention.

He looks back at the house.

The front door opens, and Stella, in her twenties, walks in. Her dark hair is in a braid, which highlights her high cheekbones and gray-green eyes. Her mother, Bee, is a pepper-haired and energetic woman.

They are midconversation and carry several grocery bags.

"And no! I will not apologize," Stella reiterates to Bee. "I was asked for my opinion, and I only gave it after specifically asking them if they *really* wanted to know it, and only after having tried to change the subject at least twice before that. Frankly, I think I did more than what's socially expected."

Bee shakes her head. "Stella, sometimes you need to consider if the person really wants your opinion or just validation."

"Well," Stella says smartly. "Maybe that person should consider if *they* want an opinion or validation."

Saint bursts in and bounds to Stella.

She kneels and throws her arms around him. "Saint! You came back!"

Bee grins. "Told you he'd come home."

Pierce and Luke walk into the house through the sliding porch door.

"He was *brought* home, actually," Pierce says.

Stella is still focused on Saint. "Yeah? By who?"

"Luke found him on the other side of the lake."

"Who's Luke?" she asks, looking up.

"I am. Nice to meet you all," Luke smiles, nodding to both Stella and Bee.

"Oh! Hi. Nice to meet you," Bee says quickly, crossing the threshold and offering her hand.

Stella nods. "How much do you want for the reward?"

Luke smiles shyly. "No, nothing."

"I've already asked him," Pierce clarifies.

"Well, won't you stay for dinner?" Bee implores.

"I've already asked him about that too." Pierce laughs.

"And I said yes," Luke admits.

"Good! It'll be great to have more company." Bee smiles.

"Well, I smell like a cigar. Pardon me while I freshen up. Luke, please help yourself to the bar."

Bee talks to Luke. "I'm Barbara—call me Bee. This is Stella."

Saint comes over and leans against Luke as if to bail him out.

"Nice to meet everyone."

Stella grabs plates and hands them to Luke. "Well, if you're staying for dinner, help me set the table."

Bee shakes her head and whispers to Luke as he walks by. "Don't take it personally. She's just got a lot of drive in her."

Stella pulls silverware from the kitchen drawer, "I'm still here. I can hear you."

Luke grins. "Oh, it's fine Mrs. Bee. She doesn't scare me much."

Stella ignores them. "What was Saint doing when you found him?"

"Well, he peed on my truck. Then ate a sandwich."

Stella and Bee burst out in laughter.

"I'm surprised he wanted to come home at all!" Bee chuckles.

Luke puts plates down on the dinner table while Stella places forks and knives.

"You should consider getting that microchip phone number updated," he says.

"Yeah," Stella frowns. "I fat-fingered the registration, then lost the information."

Bee puts out a cheese plate. "You from around here?" she asks.

"Colorado, originally."

"What're you doing up here?" she continues.

"Oh, you know, chapter two of life. Retired military and all that."

Stella's interest is piqued. "Dad was in the navy."

"Yeah, he showed me his pictures, and we shared a few stories out there on your dock." Luke points to the now-dark outdoors.

"And so we did!" Pierce trumpets upon returns. He takes a piece of bread out of Bee's hand and chews on it. "What are we having, and how can I help eat it?"

"You, mister, can help me by making this caprese salad. Are you okay with that?" Bee asks Luke.

"Absolutely."

Pierce comes over with a bottle of red wine and places glasses out.

They are filled and raised.

"Well," Pierce toasts. "Here's to us, and here's to Saint."

They all sip, then the front doorbell rings. Saint runs past Luke and knocks his leg.

Wine sloshes across Luke's shirt.

"Dammit," Luke curses. "He's like a train."

In one fluid stride, Bee gets a dish towel and tosses it to Luke, then turns to Pierce.

"Darling, that's probably Emily from next door. She said she was in town, so I invited her over. And you, Stella," she instructs. "Show Luke the bathroom and get him a shirt from your father's closet."

Pierce dutifully does as told, and Stella walks by Luke.

"You know, if you hold the glass right, you don't spill it," she chides in a whisper.

Luke registers the challenge. "Well, if you had entered your phone number right, you wouldn't be losing your dog as often."

"Kids!" Bee settles in a motherly tone.

Pierce opens the front door. Sporting dreadlocked hair, Emily is dressed in an oversized hand-knit sweater, a bottle of wine in hand. She hugs Pierce, then embraces Bee.

Luke, meanwhile, follows Stella past the kitchen and down the back hallway. Rows of photos line the wall, and Stella points to the bathroom door. He goes in and turns on the light while she goes to the master bedroom farther down.

"Seriously, thanks for saving Saint," Stella calls from the room. "He might be getting older, but he still runs off."

Luke walks up to the sink and evaluates the wine stain in the mirror. "No worries," he says. "Glad I could help."

Around the corner, Stella rummages through her father's closet. "If I can't get his number updated, I might just have to put a new chip in him."

Luke can't help but laugh, then takes his shirt off and starts to wash it with soap and hot water. "Or, you know, put a tag on his collar with your phone number on it."

Stella compares one shirt to another, then furrows her brow and whispers his comment back to herself, *"Or put my number on his collar."*

"Or call the guy in Minnesota," Luke continues, "and give him your number."

Stella has had enough of his advice and shakes her head. She chooses a shirt and walks to the bathroom with it in hand. She is about to parry his last comment with something witty when she sees Luke leaning over the sink. He is topless, and despite having retired from the military, his body is firmly in shape. His arms are well defined, and Stella can see several pock-marked holes in his upper shoulder. She considers saying something, anything, when he looks up and catches her gaze in the mirror.

"Here," she stutters, giving him the shirt. "Should fit."

Luke takes it. "Am I going to stretch it out?"

"Oh, you're fine. I mean—" She blushes. "The *shirt* will be fine."

Luke puts it on. The buttons can only fasten to the third from the top, and he loosens the cuffs. The shirt is tight but wearable.

"I feel like I should be in a boy band."

Stella can't help herself. "Backstreet or NSYNC?"

"Both were great. Hopefully I don't pop any buttons over dinner."

"It's just dinner, won't have to be doing any army roll crawls or anything."

"*Roll crawls?* Are you just making things up?"

Stella imitates crawling with her elbows. "You know… when you crawl and roll. Isn't that the first thing they teach you?"

Luke grins. "And probably the only thing, but for your information—" He stops abruptly as something in the hall catches his attention. It is a framed picture of a silver seaplane with a black horse near the red tail.

Luke brushes past Stella and walks up to it.

"This," he points. "This plane. How do you know *this* plane?"

Stella is puzzled by the quick transition and turns to address the question. She stands next to him in the hallway.

"That's me," she says, pointing at the cockpit. "Dad got me that plane when I started working for the charter company. This was my first solo flight."

Luke is confused. "This… is you?"

Stella crosses her arms. "Yeah, girls can fly, too, you know."

Emily interrupts them in the hallway.

"Murphy!" she cries warmly, giving Stella a hug. "Long time no see. You look wonderful."

Luke is hopelessly confused, "Murphy?"

Stella is in the middle of a long hug with Emily, her face partially buried by Emily's sweater.

"Yeah, Murphy is my middle name," she says over her shoulder.

Emily releases Stella and turns to Luke. "And you must be Luke, the one and only Saint savior. May I enter your space and hug you?"

Luke accepts but eyes Stella in the process. She doesn't understand his sudden change of mood and goes back to the kitchen. Soon after, Luke follows Emily out of the hall.

Bee sees him first.

"Oh, that shirt looks great on you. A bit snug but not bad."

Luke pulls the cuffs. "Thank you. But I have to go. I can't stay for dinner."

"What?" Bee exclaims, then looks at Stella. "What did you do?"

"Nothing! I got him a shirt!"

Pierce observes quietly.

Luke finds the keys to his truck in his pocket. "Thank you all, but she," he says, pointing at Stella, "almost killed me the other day."

Everyone turns to Stella.

"What? When?" Stella defends.

"When I was fishing, you came around the corner and almost killed me with your air boat!"

Stella is momentarily confused, then realizes that the man before her could be no one else but the man in the kayak. She takes a breath, then counts out her fingers as she speaks. "First, it's called a *sea*plane, and second, I dodged those geese and skipped off the water specifically *not* to kill you, or myself, *or* the geese." She crosses her arms defiantly. "So, you're welcome."

Bee comes from around the kitchen island. She hands Luke the caprese salad and hooks his elbow, "Oh, you can't leave now! This is just getting good."

Luke tells Bee the story as she pulls him into the dining room. "I was fishing, and she comes flying around the corner at two hundred miles an hour, then basically runs me over. I flipped out of my kayak and lost my rod!"

Stella smiles and stands resolutely behind her chair. "It maxes out at one fifty, and I was barely doing a hundred."

Bee seeks clarification. "So, did she actually hit you?

Luke shows a margin of error with his hands. "Almost."

Stella shrugs. "I'm just going to say it again to make sure everyone heard me. I ducked *under* a flock of geese, glanced off the water, and *still* missed you, all at a hundred miles an hour. I think it could have been much worse."

Pierce nods his approval. "Nice flying."

"Thanks, Dad."

Pierce then turns to Luke. "But I'm sorry about your fishing rod. You have my sympathies."

Emily is beaming. "Oh my, your auras are astounding."

Stella turns to Luke, arms still crossed. "There are ten rods in the garage. Please, take your pick."

Bee settles on Stella. "Oh honey, you almost killed him. I think this is about more than that."

Luke nods to Bee. "Thank you."

Bee responds kindly. "You're welcome."

Stella counters. "I am agreeing with you, Mom. And I'm making amends by offering him a fishing rod."

"But it's not about the fishing rod," Bee says.

"But it's not not about it either, right?" Stella challenges, looking at Luke.

Luke and Stella have a brief stare-off, and Emily starts clapping.

"Resolution!" Emily smiles. "I love the energy between you two."

Everyone moves to the table and takes a seat—except Luke and Stella, who remain standing and eyeing each other.

"Where should I sit?" Luke asks her.

"You're the guest. You pick," Stella retorts.

"Ladies first."

They continue to eye each other.

Sensing where this is going, Luke relents. "Knowing what I know about you, this could probably go on all night."

Stella grins. "You're not wrong."

"Well, I'm going to sit and have dinner, so as not to be rude."

"Be my guest."

Luke grins. "I *am* your guest, thank you."

He sits next to Emily, who quickly scoots very close to him, and Stella shakes her head realizing he has somehow won.

"Luke," Emily asks. "Can I see your palm?"

Luke lets his hand be taken. "Are you a palm reader?"

Bee nods and starts serving. "She is, actually. And a life coach and a conflict mitigator. Best Whitefish has to offer. And lives right next door."

Luke laughs. "Well, what does my palm say?"

Emily studies and ponders. "Oh. I've never seen this before."

"What's that?"

"See here, where it splits but comes together, then is intersected by this one? It means *strong-willed, but always has a choice*. You follow this line, and it is short and has no deviation. You follow this other one, and it is intersected and long-lasting."

"I don't know what that means," Luke confesses.

"Neither do I. Pass the salad?" Pierce chimes in.

Luke passes the bowl with his free hand. "I don't know if I'm buying it."

Emily lets go of his palm. "People dismiss what they can't understand."

Luke softens. "I'm sorry. I'm not dismissing it. I'll just say I don't understand."

Emily smiles and takes his hand back. "I think you'll be okay. This here," she says, pointing, "it looks like it stops, but if you look closer, it doesn't."

"Meaning?"

"Your friends will always see you through. Even if they fade. And I very specifically see Saint, who had been missing for days."

"But I brought him home," Luke counters.

Emily contemplatively massages his palm and lets it go. "We don't always have to *understand* the gift. Sometimes we are just meant to accept it."

* * *

Dinner is complete, plates are stacked, and Luke shakes hands with Pierce near the front threshold.

"Thanks for dinner," Luke says with genuine appreciation.

"Thank you for your company and for returning Saint. You're welcome anytime," Pierce replies.

Luke points at Stella. "I would, but I'm going to go out of my way to avoid her if that's okay with you."

Pierce laughs and claps Luke on the shoulder. "You're in luck. The plane is getting a yearly inspection. She won't be flying it for at least a day."

Luke chuckles and waves his thanks to Bee and Emily, and even Stella. "Thanks for dinner. It was a pleasure meeting you all."

Saint runs to him, and Luke gives the husky a final rub down before sending him back in the house. Pierce shuts the door, and Luke goes to his truck. He sits, alone, and confronts a mixture of emotions he hasn't felt in years.

Behind the door, Pierce looks back at Bee, "Well, he was nice."

Emily nods. "I like him. He's genuine."

Pierce notices the house is quiet, as if the energy had been dialed down. "Where's Stella?" he asks.

"Outside, I believe."

Pierce sees her and Saint out on the deck. They're watching the rising moon. Pierce grabs a blanket from a patio chest, walks out to her, and drapes it over her shoulders.

"Well, that was fun," he says knowingly.

Stella says nothing.

"What's up?"

"Nothing's up."

"I've flown a thousand hours with you. I know when something's up."

She sighs. "It's just… when I was giving him his shirt, he had a lot of scars on his shoulder. Looked like bullet holes."

Pierce nods. "Did you ask him about them?"

"No. Didn't think it was my place."

Pierce considers this for a moment. "In my experience, asking is better than not." He leans down and pets Saint. "And the scars aren't always physical, you know."

Stella pulls the blanket closer but says nothing.

Chapter 4

The next morning, Luke comes out of his cabin. He carries a cup of hot coffee, and the steam travels with him as he walks along the porch. He looks around, then down at the rocking chair and the empty dog bowl beside it. His eyes narrow, and he shakes his head ever so slightly. Determined to find a distraction, he places the coffee on the rail and goes to the truck. He lifts the wood from the bed and resolves to stay busy.

The day is a series of activities and sounds — sawing, drilling, and classic rock. He stops midday and walks out of the cabin, gleaming with a sheen of sweat. His arms are covered in sawdust, and he carries a sandwich. He takes a bite, looks down at Saint's old food bowl, and stops chewing because the bread tastes like cardboard.

Unable to eat any more, he tosses the rest of the sandwich into the bowl.

* * *

Later that night, Luke is inside his cabin. The fire flickers, and he sits in his old cozy chair while thumbing through a book. A metal scraping noise from the front porch catches his attention, and he recognizes it as the metal food bowl. He gets up quickly, turns the porch light on, and opens the door.

"Saint?"

A raccoon has the sandwich in its paws and is frozen in fright.

Luke shakes his head and shuts the door. He stands in the living room for a moment and looks around, then sees the truck keys on the nightstand and scoops them up.

* * *

The headlights illuminate the road ahead of him. He tunes the radio to find something to listen to, but nothing pacifies his frustration. Up ahead, he sees a flash of white on the side of the road and slows down. He passes a pair of whitetail deer, smacks the steering wheel, and keeps driving.

*   *   *

Luke pulls up to a bar on the side of the road. The logo is a pair of crossed axes, the parking lot is full, and music plays through the open windows. Luke strides in. The walls are covered in wood planks and vintage metal signs. High-top tables are in the center, and booths line the side. A dark wood bar runs one length of the room. In the backyard, which is enclosed by a chain-link fence and rimmed with strings of lights, a few people heave axes over their heads at bright targets. They laugh and joke in various crescendos.

Luke finds a seat at the bar, and Crail, wearing an apron and drying a beer glass, comes up to him.

"Long time no see!" Crail welcomes.

Luke looks over his shoulder. "What's the insurance rate on axe throwing, anyways?"

"Surprisingly nothing if they voluntarily sign away all their rights. But I took your advice and put up some loose chain link fence just in case."

A *thunk* and a cheer rise from the back; someone just hit a bullseye.

"What can I get you?" Crail asks.

Luke turns back to the bar. "Can I have a beer and fries?"

Crail pours a beer and hands it to Luke. "And a burger. Coming right up," he says, then goes to the kitchen.

A blonde woman from one of the high-top tables walks up to the bar and stands next to Luke. Her eyes are striking, and she likely gets the type of attention from men she doesn't much care for. Crail tells the cooks to make another burger, then comes back over.

"A beer, please," she asks in a heavy accent.

Luke pays attention.

Crail asks, "What kind?"

"Oh… beer. Light. Please."

Crail nods and pours her one.

"How much dollars?" she asks.

"Four," Crail responds, showing her four fingers.

Luke leans over. *"Ot'kuda vi?"*

She looks back at Luke with surprise. *"Ukraine, Kievi. A ty?"*

"Ya z' Ameriki."

"A vy govoritie po Ruskie?"

Luke grins and makes a small symbol with his finger, *"Chyut-chyut. A shto vy deli-esh zdies?"* [A little bit. And what are you doing here?]

She grins and moves her hair behind her ear. "Language work exchange. With the ski hotel."

"Not bad."

Her girlfriends materialize at her side. *"Ho-ch Nika, mi gra'hmi."* [Come Nika, we're playing.]

Nika looks at Luke. "This axing throw, is this big American sport?"

Luke watches her friends. They are signing waivers. "I've never done it, but it looks like fun."

Nika grins and pauses, but the expected ask for her phone number or request to join does not come. Not one to let an opportunity pass, she cuts to the point. "Can you take my phone number?"

Luke shrugs. "Sure."

Nika smiles and writes her number down on the back of a coaster. Crail watches this exchange with interest and amusement.

"Za'dzwoin menya," she says, handing him her number.

Luke nods, and Crail waits until she leaves.

"And you speak Russian?" he asks.

"Some, not all."

Crail looks back at Nika. "Looks like you speak enough."

Luke puts his empty glass on the phone-numbered coaster and pushes it to Crail. "All yours if you want it."

"Even if I *were* single, I'm quite sure I wouldn't know what to do with her."

Luke laughs and Crail gets him another beer.

"How's life?" Crail asks.

"Hmm…" Luke muses. "Where to start?"

"Cabin good?"

"Cabin's good."

"Truck?"

"It runs."

"The dog?"

There's a pause. "Returned him."

"Hmm."

"Anything else?"

"What else do you want to talk about?"

Luke chuckles. "I'm going to the bathroom."

He pushes back from the bar and walks down the hall.

While using the urinal, he reads a bathroom advertisement

about horseback riding and glamping. He wonders if he could be a ranch hand on a farm somewhere, then makes his way back to the bar. His seat is reserved by his basket of fries. Then he notices, suspects, and confirms that it is no one else but Stella standing next to them.

"Really?" he asks, genuinely inquisitive.

Stella turns and sees him. "Are you following me?" she asks with suspicion.

"I'm pretty sure I was here first."

"No, I got here a few minutes ago."

Luke reaches over and eats a fry. "And I got here a few minutes before that."

She looks at the basket, takes a fry, and bites it. "They're warm… so maybe you're not lying."

Luke chuckles. "No reason to lie. How's Saint?"

Crail comes up to them. "What can I get you?"

She asks for a beer, and Crail asks for an ID in return. She gives it to him, and he tries to find her birthday but can't read the numbers due to his bad eyes and low light.

Luke sees him struggling. "She's good, I'll vouch for her."

Stella is surprised. "Will you now?"

Crail puts the ID down. "You know her?"

Luke nods slowly but says nothing more.

Crail is hailed by a kitchen staff member and quickly pours a beer. "Well, if he says you're good, you're good." He gives it to her and rushes back.

"Thank you," she tells Crail, then looks at Luke. "Saint is fine."

"What brings you here?" he asks.

"Emily came over to figure out if dogs could have their paws read. I had to go."

Luke laughs. "She's quite the mystic."

"And we both ended up here?" She laughs, then makes air-quotes. "That's pretty *mystical* if you ask me."

Luke weighs this idea. "In our collective defense, there's only one bar on this end of the lake."

"You're saying you don't believe in destiny?"

Luke sighs. "Copernicus effect."

"What?"

"It's when people think things happen to just *them*, and they can't fathom examples proving the opposite. It's called the Copernicus effect."

She looks at him with interest. "You're going to have to explain that a little more."

Luke takes a sip of his beer. "Since everyone is the center of their own lives, then by default, people see events happening to no one else but them. It's incomprehensible for a simple person to believe that they might be wholly inconsequential to the event, or even the universe. It's a mental fallacy of self-importance."

Stella crosses her arms. "Who came up with that idea?"

Luke shrugs as his burger is delivered. "I did."

Stella eats another one of his fries. "Well, if I must admit, I did see your truck. Thought I recognized it."

Luke says nothing, and a silence develops between them. They are distracted by a group of people celebrating a flawed axe throw.

"So," Stella asks, "axe throwing?"

Luke nods toward Crail, who is working on removing an order from a server's bill. "Yeah, he wanted more customers, so we brainstormed over beers in his backyard."

Crail sees Luke looking at him and comes over. "You guys doing okay?"

Stella points at Luke. "He's saying the axe throwing was all his idea."

Luke pushes her hand down. "No, I didn't! I just challenged him to throw an axe at a tree stump one evening, and he stuck it from ten feet away."

Stella is impressed. "Did you now?"

Crail laughs. "I was as surprised as you are."

Stella looks around and takes another sip. She sees an axe throwing booth wrapping up, the occupants high-fiving each other with finality.

"So, are we going to throw a few?" she asks, eyebrows raised.

Luke looks at her, then at the throwing lane. "Hmm, not sure."

Crail watches this exchange, and in a moment of realization, coughs. *"Snowmobile."*

Stella turns. "Excuse me?"

"Oh, just got a tickle in my throat… *Snowmobile!*" He coughs again, this time more forcefully.

"Really?" she says, not buying it. "Because it sounds like you're saying 'snowmobile.'"

Luke catches on and looks at Crail. "Yeah? Really? Now?"

Crail nods. "Yeah. Really. And since it's your first time, we're running a special. It's on the house. So, go. *Now.*"

Stella looks at Luke and knows something has transpired but is not sure what. "Well, are we doing this?" she asks.

Luke gives a reluctant shake of the head, but Crail is having none of it.

"Snow-mo-bile," he enunciates.

Luke purses his lips. He briefly weighs their agreement and chooses to respect their pact on principle. "Yeah, yeah, let's go throw some axes," he says with a frustrated double-palm slap on the bar. "Why not?"

Stella is still highly suspicious of the exchange between them but decides to let it go. She takes her beer and heads to the throwing booth. Luke follows, then looks back and points a finger at Crail for using their safe word so soon.

Crail points a finger in return and throws a bar towel his way. "Snowmobile!" he says with a grin.

Stella and Luke approach the attendant by the chain-link fence and fill out the necessary waivers.

"Crail said we're on the house," Luke lets the attendant know. "So here," he says, offering a hearty tip.

The attendant smiles gratefully and takes them to an open lane. They pass Nika and her group. In the tight confines, Luke walks past Nika, and she turns toward him, interpreting his presence as a desire to talk to her. Nika then sees Stella and is less than enthused.

The attendant talks to Luke and Stella as they walk. "One axe at a time, one thrower on the line. Don't catch the axe if it jumps back. And have fun!"

Luke picks a few axes from the wall. "Have you ever thrown an axe?" he asks Stella.

"Can't say that I have," she admits.

"Well, there's a lot of science, or you could learn by doing. What's your preference?"

She holds an axe and feels the heft of the handle. "I learn by doing." She takes a moment to study the group throwing next to them, then tries to replicate their overhead double-hand throw technique. Stella misses the bullseye, and the blade doesn't stick in the plywood backing, but she makes an audible *ha!* in satisfaction.

Luke takes a smaller axe, steps to the line, and throws it with one hand. It sticks low and off-center.

Stella gives him a look.

"Beginner's luck, I swear," he says.

She imitates Crail and points a finger at him. "There's humility, and then there's bragging. Which one are you doing right now?"

"Neither," Luke grins. "I'm just here for the beer."

"All right, let's see what I can do," she says, feeling the warmth of a good-natured competition grow between them. She picks a double-headed axe, takes a practice swing, and throws. The handle hits the target and bounces off the backstop.

"Dammit," she whispers.

Luke hands her another axe. "I think you're in the middle of your rotation. Take one baby step forward."

Stella looks at her feet, does as instructed, and makes another throw.

It sticks.

"Ha!" she exclaims louder, delighted.

Luke gives her a high five and walks to the throw line. He tosses his, and it sticks into the backboard.

"So, how'd Saint lose his leg?" he asks.

"Dog sledding," she says without pause.

"Really?"

"Yeah. I wanted to do the Beargrease. He was my point." Stella steps up with a new axe, and Luke comes over and adjusts her grip.

"It'll release better if you relax these fingers. And… what does bear grease do for a dog sled? Does it cut down on the friction?"

Stella is confused. "Beargrease for the sled? Ha! No, no. It's the name of a dog sled race in northern Minnesota." She turns her attention back to the target. "The John Beargrease, up Lake Superior almost to the Canadian border. Second only to the Iditarod. Dad had this crazy idea that I could be the first girl to win it. And I almost did." She throws and sticks the target. She is happy but notices that Luke's presence has shifted.

Luke is eyeing a situation in the bar. A bro in a designer trucker hat is harassing Nika and her group of friends. Hat-Bro drapes an arm around Nika, and she shrugs it off, but he persists. It is clear to Luke that Hat-Bro is only charming himself.

Luke puts his beer to the side. "Give me one second, will you?" he says, then leaves the chain-link fence area and walks briskly back into the bar.

One of Nika's friends has managed to convince Hat-Bro to leave them alone, and he grudgingly does so. Hat-Bro regroups with his other bro buddy, and they commiserate about why they weren't successful, which in their minds has everything to do with everyone else and nothing to do with them.

Luke comes up to Nika. "Everything okay?"

Nika is bristling with annoyance at the bros, but when she sees Luke, her demeanor softens. "Yes. Thank you. Just this jerk," she says with a point of her thumb.

"Excuse me?" Hat-Bro says loudly, having clearly heard the *jerk* comment.

Luke speaks to the bro table. "She's entitled to her opinion."

"Is there a problem?" Hat-Bro asks Luke.

Luke shakes his head. "Not at the moment." He then addresses Nika directly, *"Ty-moi sestra,"* before turning back to the bro table. "But if you keep harassing my sister, I will make it a problem."

Hat-Bro realizes he's violated the Bro Code and settles down. "Oh, sorry, bro. I didn't know."

"Just keep it civil, okay?"

"Okay, okay."

Luke smiles, nods to Nika, and starts to walk away. It is then that Nika chooses to take it a step further.

"Yeah! Or my brother will kick your stupid asshole!" she exclaims.

This is all the justification the bros need. After all, they had flown in from LA and hadn't timed the ski season right, so they were bored, antsy, and looking to blame someone else.

"Oh, will he now?" Hat-Bro asks.

"Yes, you bitch-head!" Nika sneers.

Luke stops walking, looks at Stella, and shakes his head. He turns to face the tables and readdresses the bros. "No, no I'm not. I'm here to have a quiet night and to make sure we all act like adults."

Hat-Bro walks up to Luke and closes the distance. "Yeah? Or what?"

Luke frowns. *"Or what?* What does that even mean?"

The brim of Hat-Bro's hat dances in front of Luke's face. It is meant to be an intentional taunt, and Hat-Bro tries to tap Luke on the bridge of the nose with it.

"It means I'm going to kick your ass," Hat-Bro snarls slowly, the smell of onion rings occluding the air between them.

The moment simmers.

"Your hat," Luke whispers, "is really stupid."

Luke sees Hat-Bro's fist clench, nose flare, and body shift back. Hat-Bro telegraphs his swing and tries to deliver a sloppy haymaker. Luke steps back and lets the punch pass, grabs the wrist, and wraps Hat-Bro's arm around his own neck.

Luke holds Hat-Bro in place and leans into his ear. "Walk out. Don't fight it," he says calmly.

"Man! Fuck you!" Hat-Bro spits.

Luke tightens his grip, and Hat-Bro is alarmed that he can no longer breathe. Luke whispers again, "Do what I say, or this is the end of the road for you and your dumb hat."

Hat-Bro makes himself compliant and, like a confused cat held by the scruff, is moved to the front door. Stella watches all this from the backyard and sees Hat-Bro's friend grab a beer bottle. He lifts it up and moves behind Luke.

"Luke! Duck!" Stella shouts.

Luke crunches down and turns Hat-Bro around. The beer bottle bounces off Hat-Bro's head in a dull thud, and he collapses like a heavy sack of potatoes. Luke makes no effort to keep him up and lets him fall.

He looks at the other bro. "What did you do that for?"

Several concerns race through Hat-Bro's-Friend's mind. They range from not wanting to get punched in the face to not wanting to get in trouble and having to tell his parents.

Down on the floor, Hat-Bro starts to snore.

Luke glances down at him, "Great, now you have to take him to the hospital."

Overwhelmed, Hat-Bro's-Friend flees the bar. Luke watches him run out and feels the abandonment of their bro-lationship. He is fundamentally annoyed.

"Oh, come on! You're just going to leave him like this?!" he shouts after him.

Crail comes over and hands Luke a six-pack of beer. "One of the waitresses called the cops, so it's time to go."

Luke takes the beer. "Appreciate it." He then turns to Stella, who has approached from outside. "You ready?" he asks.

She nods and smiles politely at Crail. "Nice to meet you."

"You too," Crail says, ushering them out the back door.

"Are you good to handle all this?" Luke asks over his shoulder.

Crail nods. "Not the first fight, won't be the last."

* * *

Luke's tailgate is down, and he and Stella sit on the back of the truck. They are parked along the lake's edge, and the moon reflects off the still water. The stars twinkle in the sky but do not reflect off the black glass, as if having chosen to limit their existence to only one showing.

Stella giggles midstory. "And then *thonk!*" She imitates someone falling and starts laughing again before experiencing a wash of concern. "Oh my God. What if he died?"

Luke pulls out a few blankets from the storage case in the bed of the truck and hands one to her. "It wasn't that hard of a hit, was it? More like a tap. But yeah, if he did get seriously injured, I'm sure Crail would have called by now."

He takes two beer bottles from the six-pack and tries to pry them open. Much to his frustration, he can't get them to budge.

"I, uh, think those are twist-offs," Stella teases.

Luke looks at the beers. He twists the tops and hands one to Stella. "I was just making sure they weren't *not* twist-offs."

She grins. "Yeah, because that makes total sense."

Luke wraps himself in a blanket. They sit quietly while the radio plays softly from the cab of the truck.

"I biffed a turn," Stella finally says.

"What?"

"Saint. That's how he lost his leg. I miscalculated a turn."

"Oh."

"I tumbled off the sled, the dogs stopped and waited for me, but the next sledder came around the corner fast and… and they tried to avoid me, but they slid over and took Saint out. It…. it wasn't good."

Luke sips his beer. "It never is."

"I think it would be easier if he held a grudge."

"I don't think dogs hold grudges."

"Well, do wolves? He's half."

Luke grins. "Maybe that's why he keeps running off."

"Oh, stop it!" she says, smacking his thigh. "Saint has the biggest heart in the world."

"The world could use more dogs like him."

Stella is quiet. She looks out and takes in the view. Her blanket has shifted off her shoulder and Luke lifts it and covers her back up.

She looks over at him. "I've been meaning to ask. What happened?"

"With?"

"Your shoulder."

"Hmm."

"Did you get shot?"

Luke nods. "Only a few times."

She shakes her head and imitates him. *"Only a few times."*

"Desperado" by the Eagles starts to play on the radio.

They listen to it for a minute, and Luke gets up, walks to the cab of the truck, and turns it off.

Stella waits for him to come back around. "Good choice. No one likes that song."

Luke laughs but doesn't sit back down on the tailgate. Instead, he picks up a rock and throws it into the water.

The stillness is broken, and the undulations create reflected moon rings.

Stella says nothing.

"I was in Afghanistan. Late-night mission," he says as if speaking to no one.

He throws another rock into the water. They watch it splash, and he doesn't speak again until the ripples dissipate.

"I enlisted with Kyle," Luke sighs. "We went into Special Forces together."

"What's Special Forces?"

"Army SF. Green Berets."

"Oh," she says quietly, not too sure what *Special Forces* entails.

Luke picks up on her pause and offers a simple explanation. "We work with the resistance, train and advise them, force multiply. Answer questions for policymakers, create options. You know, things like that."

Stella nods but doesn't have any idea how those things are at all related.

Luke smiles, remembering. "Kyle and I grew up together. Learned to ride bikes, went camping and fishing.… you know. No matter what we did, though, he always had this ear-to-ear grin. And a huge mop of red hair. Never in regs. Got yelled at all the time."

There's a pause as if Luke is trying to separate a strong memory from an even deeper emotion. He laughs to himself before continuing the story.

"He always said 'Go for broke' when the situation got crazy." Luke shakes his head. "During selection, he looks at me and tells me he has to get some sleep or he's going to fall over standing up. He sees the air vent to a huge air-conditioning unit, and he undoes it and crawls into it to sneak some sleep. The instructor comes in and starts yelling for accountability, and I had to cause a distraction so Kyle could sneak back out and not get caught. I acted like I had a massive cramp in my leg and fell over on the cadre." He chuckles but says nothing else for quite some time.

"Last year," he picks back up, "we were leading our partner element through a compound in Afghanistan, and we started taking fire. Kyle and I see a building, and we rush to take the top floor. Last room, I turn left, and one of our Afghan brothers, Safi, turns right. Safi gets shot in the chest by an AK on full auto. I get hit in the shoulder by the rounds after they pass through him. Kyle comes in number three and shoots the guy, but somehow ends up taking a round through the ankle."

Luke starts laughing and quickly wipes a welling tear. "I think it was a damn ricochet. And so we're up there, and Kyle is throwing a dressing on me while hopping around, cursing it. 'A ricochet? A goddamn ricochet?' And I'm laughing too — but, you know, my shoulder and Safi. So, we're laughing, but also sad that Safi is messed up. Then an RPG comes screaming by. Misses the window by just a few inches. Kyle yells for me to get Safi out of there while he covers us. I get maybe a few feet out of that door when…"

Luke pauses, remembering the concussion and the flash of orange.

"Another RPG came in and exploded in the room," he starts back up. "I don't really remember anything after that. I had a bad concussion for days. They offered me a desk job once I recovered… but I just couldn't. So, I asked for a medical retirement, and that was that."

* * *

A few miles from Fort Bragg, North Carolina, a faded taxi turns into a well-kept neighborhood. It drives along and passes several well-to-do homes. The houses have neatly clipped lawns, and a few bicycles have been left on the driveways even though unattended bicycles are a clear violation of HOA bylaws. Parking a car in the driveway is another violation, Rule 47 to be exact, which states that "all cars must be parked in the garage with the garage door shut, or on the street." But most everyone ignores Rule 47, especially the Millers. They park their new car with dealer plates in the driveway to make sure the Smiths can see it, because the two families have been engaged in a passive-aggressive middle-class duel for years. Two years ago, it was above-ground pools, last year it was backyard swing sets, and this year it's new cars.

High above the repetitive rooflines and displays of personal success, the sun has set, and down below, the taxi has found its destination. It stops in front of a home, and a tired man gets out. He has a beard that is several months old, and one of his arms is in a black sling. He pulls out a backpack, shoulders it on his good side, and pays the fare. The taxi driver instinctively hands him a receipt but doesn't say anything.

The taxi pulls away, and the Bearded Man stands there, alone. None of the neighbors see him, and even if they had, they wouldn't have known what to say other than "Oh, you're back again?" while wondering if he would finally get around to mowing his lawn.

Because they forgot his name or never knew it in the first place.

The Bearded Man turns and looks at the front of his house. The lights are off, and the grass is a foot tall, which was to be expected since his fiancée left him three months ago. An email explained that she couldn't continue being with a man who was never home, and this explanation was followed by a list of important events missed, anger that he was "more married to his job than he would be to her," and comments that "he was always a different man when he came home." The email continued for several more paragraphs, but he hadn't bothered to read those.

Amanda.

He didn't blame her, though, because all those things were essentially true. In their two years of being together, he had only been home six months, and even those had been inconsistent.

Two or three weeks there, a month or two here.

The wedding had been postponed twice, then officially called off until things "settled down." Ironically, he had logged over a hundred thousand frequent flier miles traveling from his home but had rarely been in it. He tried to remember Amanda's face, but like the sun above, that too had faded.

She was a good catch. She'll find someone new.

Alone, the Bearded Man walks to his house and reaches for the front door. The doorknob turns but doesn't open, and he realizes he doesn't have any idea where his house keys are. If they weren't in his backpack, then they were at the bottom of a tuff box in Afghanistan.

He opens the zipper pouch of the backpack and rummages through various items. An iPod, a book, flight itineraries, travel orders, an official passport, and a team picture of everyone standing in front of two Gun-Vees spills out. The photo had been taken at the end of a four-day, nonstop operation—one of many. They had cleared every insurgent and blown every cache in their area of operation.

He looks at the weary smiles on his team's faces. They're all grinning.

The picture reminds him of the simple completeness of it all, one where the metrics of life are clearer and every color more defined. The heat, sand, explosions, people, sweat, blood, laughter, and tears were vividly palpable. Despite the constant presence of death, or perhaps because of it, he felt more alive in a day there than he would in a year back home.

He looks at the picture a moment longer. He is proud to be a man among men, a warrior among warriors, and wouldn't trade his bad hip, fractured rib, or injured shoulder for any of it.

He sees Kyle standing next to him in the photo.

But he'd trade everything for him.

Then, as if deployed, the Bearded Man's weary attention snaps back to the mission at hand—finding house keys he hadn't seen in six months.

He rummages around in another pouch.

Nothing.

But he does find his cellphone.

Even though he and Amanda had broken up, the engagement ring having sat on the kitchen counter for the past few months, he wonders whether he can call her and ask her if she still has a spare key.

And maybe dinner?

He presses the power button, but the phone's battery is dead. Months in the summer heat has cooked it like a cockroach. He tosses the phone in the backpack and reassesses the situation. As he does so, the streetlights behind him start to click on. The HOA installed energy-efficient lights while he had been gone because that had been the most pressing issue at the time.

Without a key or a phone, the Bearded Man seeks an alternate plan. He walks around the side of his house and casually registers that the grass is taller. A few tree branches are littered about, likely from the last storm, and he steps onto the wooden deck that hasn't been used since last summer. He sees that his once-new grill is rusted, and he passes it to peer through the kitchen window. The green microwave clock blinks on and off, but the house is otherwise unlit. He tries the back door, but it doesn't open, and he briefly wonders why he hadn't hidden a key under the mat.

Because I expected to come home to a fiancée.

Frustrated, he looks at the rusty grill. He opens it and, inside, sees a set of grilling tools. He picks up the spatula and wonders whether he could use the flat metal end to pry the window jab open. Without any other option, he jams the metal face between the windowpanes but achieves nothing. A frustrated minute later, he flips the spatula around and breaks the window with the handle. The glass cracks and he plucks the shards out one by one. He brushes the edges of the window with the grill scrubber and, with the glass cleared, unlatches the window before opening it.

He is greeted by the beeping of the home alarm.

`Fault zone two. Fault zone two.`

At least she set the alarm.

He expertly slides through the window but cuts his finger on an errant shard. He walks to the alarm console and flips the cover. The backlit buttons light up.

What's my code?

He lifts a finger and pauses. He feels like a bomb-disposal technician who doesn't know which wire to cut, but with time counting down, he enters a series of numbers that seem vaguely familiar.

The console rejects them angrily.

`Incorrect code entered.`

He tries another variation, the numbers feeling more foreign as he does so.

```
Incorrect code entered.

Incorrect code entered.

Incorrect code entered.
```

He watches the timer count down, and like the bomb technician, accepts the inevitable.

"The hell with it," he says out loud.

He leaves the beeping console and turns to the refrigerator. He opens the freezer and is comforted to see a bottle of whiskey loyally and selflessly sitting in the back. It is fully coated in a thick sheet of frost. He picks it up, his fingertips melt through the ice, and in that grip, many months of loneliness end for the both of them.

The alarm, ignorant of the Bearded Man's homecoming, reaches zero and blares a warbling squeal. It sends a message to the security monitoring service that the house has had a potential break-in, and the technician on duty calls the number on file, which is to the Bearded Man's dead phone in his backpack. There is no answer. The technician then calls the second number on file—Amanda's—but she doesn't recognize the number and doesn't answer it. Per protocol, the technician calls the local police and informs them of the possible intrusion. While the technician routes the address to the dispatcher, the

Bearded Man, open bottle in hand, grows more and more annoyed at the warbling alarm. He has spent months doing what had to be done to achieve mission success, and still in that mindset, he opens the kitchen drawer and pulls out a steak knife.

Ten minutes later, two uniformed police officers approach the Bearded Man's house. The lights are on, and the front door shows no signs of a break-in. The Senior Officer suspects it is a case of a forgotten code but approaches the door with professional caution. He instructs the Junior Officer to walk around the house but not enter, primarily because the Junior, younger in age and experience, has demonstrated himself to be prone to adrenaline rushes, accusations, and animated stories at barbecue parties. This is also his first home-invasion call.

The Senior Officer knocks on the front door.

There is a shuffle from inside the house but no response.

The Senior knocks again, "Police, we received a report of a break-in."

The Junior Officer returns to the front of the house. He is out of breath. He saw the broken window but, too flustered to radio it in, ran as fast as he could to the front.

A bearded, muscular, shirtless, arm-slung, and shoeless man opens the front door. He stands quietly on the threshold with a bottle in one hand and a paper towel wrapped around a bloody finger on the other. Cake's "The Distance" plays in the background, and the faint smell of whiskey floats through the door.

The Senior Officer steps back. "Sir, are you the owner of this house?"

The Bearded Man nods. "I am."

"We received a report of your home alarm having gone off."

The Bearded Man looks behind him at the alarm console. The lights are blinking, but the steak knife, which is buried into the console's speaker, has done its job.

"I forgot my code," he says flatly.

"The security company tried to call you. Why didn't you answer?" the Junior interjects, annoyed at the drunk.

The Bearded Man looks at the younger officer. It is a cold and blank evaluation. The Junior doesn't know what he is seeing, but the Senior does. He had seen his friends come back with the same look after Vietnam.

"My phone isn't working, so I didn't get the call," the Bearded Man says calmly.

The Senior Officer steps in. "Sir, do you have any identification?"

The Bearded Man continues to look at the Junior Officer. He wonders what the Junior's last thoughts would be if he took his pistol and turned it around on him. And more so, would the Junior's wife, children, and parents really believe that, in his last moments, their husband, father, and son protected and served the community he loved?

The Bearded Man takes a slow swig of whiskey and looks back at the Senior Officer. The older cop has more sense about him, and the Bearded Man makes the conscious decision to return to the civilian world and play by civilian rules.

Same team.

He slowly points the bottle toward his living room. "My ID is in my backpack, over there next to the couch. I have to go get it and dig around. There's nothing dangerous in there."

The Senior looks at the Junior Officer. This was not their normal procedure, as they were used to dictating the situation. "Well, how about you get the backpack, bring it out here, and open it on the porch. It'll be safer for all involved."

The Bearded Man, who has kicked in more doors and conducted more raids than he could count, nods in polite compliance. He leaves the door open, and the Junior moves his hand to the butt of his gun, just in case. He watches with focused intensity as the Bearded Man gets the backpack and returns to the front stoop. Once there, he sits down in the doorway while flanked by both cops. He digs around for his wallet and pulls each item out slowly. He places them in a neat row next to him as not to startle the officers—a Kindle, military orders, an old iPod. The wallet is found, and the man pulls out his military ID. He holds it out, and when the Junior Officer reaches for it, the Bearded Man moves it away and hands it to the Senior.

The Junior Officer's ego is hurt, but he refuses to show it.

"Give me a minute while I call this in," the Senior says as he walks back to the squad car.

No longer constrained, the Junior Officer looks at the man sitting in front of him. "What kind of guy gets so drunk he forgets his house code?" he asks, still stinging from being marginalized.

The Bearded Man takes another swig of the bottle. "I'm not drunk… yet."

The Junior tries to think of something else to say and looks down at the backpack. He sees the edge of a picture sticking out, and the sight of more than a few rifles catches his attention. He is an avid turkey hunter himself and always reads hunting magazines. He recognizes the rifles to be M4s, and curiously, like a child, he reaches down to pick up the photo.

The Bearded Man imagines monkey-wrapping himself around the Junior's exposed head and choking him out until the job is done.

"What's this?" the Junior asks, standing up and inspecting the picture.

Every guy in the photo has a rifle, a pistol, and more than enough kit to outfit a much larger unit. The Junior reasoned they were better equipped than the local SWAT team, and on top of that, each Humvee had two machine guns on their back tailgates, a minigun in the turret of one, and what looked like a stubby grenade launcher in the other.

And they all looked so proud.

"It's a picture," the Bearded Man says calmly, still sitting.

"I know *that*," the Junior snaps, unwittingly getting sucked into the Bearded Man's mind games. He then recognizes one of the men in the photo to be the shirtless man sitting in front of him.

"Is this you?" he asks, pointing to the guy standing on the hood of the truck.

The Senior comes back and gives the Bearded Man his ID, as well as a yellow sticky note. "Sorry for the inconvenience. I explained your situation, confirmed your identity, and all they asked is that you call them back to update your information. I wrote your access code down on the note."

The Bearded Man, now severely tired, looks at the sticky note. "Thank you. I appreciate it."

The Senior nods slightly, knowing that muscles and striations like the Bearded Man's were only gained after years of serious work. He also knows that the whiskey-drinking calmness and hollow eyes mask the depth of things he has seen and done. The Senior looks over at his

Junior, who is still holding the picture, and takes it from him.

He returns it to the rightful owner. "Sorry for the confusion," the Senior continues. "And thank you for your cooperation." The Senior Officer then notices that the music has stopped playing and the house is quiet, completely absent of friends and family. "And for what it's worth… welcome home."

The Bearded Man nods but says nothing. He stays seated while the cops leave, then looks at the photo and realizes, with the stark finality of truth, that the picture *is* a picture of home. His family reunions were handshakes in foreign countries with focused and like-minded fighters, with M4s, Glocks, knives, grenades, and flashbangs as accessories. Instead of politely asking about kids or talking about taxes while serving potato casserole, their conversations were about who was still alive, who had died, and how they could do more for the greater good.

The Bearded Man looks at the man standing next to him in the photo. He has an ear-to-ear grin, and a lock of red hair crests his forehead.

Kyle.

And so, it was here, on the front stoop of an empty house, with civilians who were worried about putting the recycling out on time and making sure their streetlamps were energy efficient, that he felt most like a stranger.

* * *

Luke tosses another rock into the lake. "Anyways," he says. "Got out, sold the house, and didn't stop till I got here."

Stella nods. "And now that you're here, what are you doing?"

"I got a cabin. Remodeling it"

She shakes her head. "How's fishing going?"

He shrugs. "It's something to do."

Stella eyes Luke. "For the rest of your life?"

He humphs but says nothing.

"Ever heard of surrogate activities?"

Luke chuckles. "Can't say I have."

"They're things we do to distract ourselves from what we were meant to do."

"Are you saying I'm not much of a fisherman?"

She laughs. "You need challenges. Daily efforts. Purpose."

"So?"

"So now that you're here, what's your next challenge going to be?"

He stoops down and picks up another rock. He is about to throw it when he pauses. "You're serious? This isn't just some dumb first date question?"

Stella looks at Luke squarely. "This isn't a date. And yes, it's a serious question."

Luke looks around. He half-heartedly tosses the rock, and it disappears in the water.

"Teach me how to fly?"

"Is that a question or a statement?" Stella challenges.

He registers the subtle change in her voice. It strikes a chord with him, and she watches him think it through.

"It's a statement," Luke says.

Chapter 5

Bee reads the morning paper and sips coffee. Stella walks into the kitchen and looks around the island. She looks frustrated.

"What did you lose?" Bee asks.

"My ID, I can't find it."

"Did you have it last night?"

Stella thinks for a moment. "Yes, at the bar. I showed it to the bartender."

"Oh? You went out?"

Stella counters her mother's mischief. "And I threw a few axes, thank you very much for asking."

"Axe throwing? Things sure have changed since my days. Did you have fun?"

Stella reflects. "You know, I did. Luke was there."

"Luke?" Bee asks excitedly. "You mean good-looking, funny, confident Luke?"

Stella blushes. "Just Luke. *Normal* Luke. Yes."

Bee shakes her head. "If that's what you think, then you're going to look back on this moment and be a very disappointed middle-aged woman. When are you seeing him again?"

"Mom!"

"Hey, okay—your life, your business," Bee says, returning to her paper.

Stella sighs. She pulls out some cereal and pours herself a bowl. She can feel her mother's patience winning. "If you must know, I'm going to see him later this morning."

"Hmm," Bee murmurs, acting disinterested.

"I'm teaching him how to fly. But I don't want to hear anything from you or Dad about it."

Bee looks at Stella with astonishment but composes herself. She thinks for a moment. "Well, best find your ID then, hmm?"

"I reckon I should."

* * *

Stella pulls up to Crail's bar. One other car is parked in the lot, but the front door is locked, and no one answers after she knocks. Undeterred, she walks to the back. The back door is propped open with a beer crate, and classic rock wafts from inside.

"Hello?" she calls. No one answers.

Stella walks in, past the beer cooler, and comes to the bar area. Crail is stocking bottles and rocking out to the music.

"Hi," Stella says.

"Oh Jesus!" he shouts in a startle. "We don't open till one."

Stella holds up her hands apologetically. "I'm sorry, the front door is closed. I knocked."

Crail recognizes her. "Wait, you're the girl from last night."

"Yes. I was here with Luke. How did the fight end up?"

Crail grins. "Went to the local clinic, just had a concussion." He then raises his eyebrows. "How about you and Luke? How did that go?"

"We had a very lovely night. I bet he'll tell you all about it."

"Oh, not so sure. He's not one to talk."

"No? Oh. I'm Stella by the way. I didn't get your name."

They shake hands. "Crail. Nice to meet you officially. Well, did he at least make it home okay?"

"I think so. He dropped me off here, and I went home on my own. But I'm seeing him soon and need my ID. Any chance I left it here?"

Crail pulls out a small box from beside the register. He thumbs through a few forgotten credit cards and IDs, then finds hers. "And here you go."

"Oh, thank you so much. Hard to fly without an ID."

"You guys are going flying?"

"Yeah."

"Like a date?"

Stella turns to leave but stops. "No… or, maybe. I don't know. Hey, can I ask you something? How well do you know him?"

Crail scratches his head. "How well does anyone know Luke?"

"What do you mean?"

He sighs. "Luke… he came into the bar one night. I tried to make conversation, but he wasn't in the mood.

But he kept coming in night after night. After about a week I got his name. After about two, I got what he was doing here. Then he starts telling me stories. He, um, he's been through some things."

"Like, because he was in the army?"

"You know, I've asked some of my retired buddies about their time in the service, and… Luke's done some things that normal infantry guys don't."

Stella cocks her head, interested.

Crail points to where Luke had been sitting the night before. "I mean, the guy speaks Russian, did you know that?"

"What? No. Why Russian?"

Crail shrugs. "Army taught him. Taught him how to drive all sorts of cars too. And jump out of planes. And other things. He once said something about having two passports. I once asked him what uniform he wore when he traveled, and he just chuckled."

Crail thinks of the many times Luke deflected questions. "Normally he just changes the subject, but when he finally gets around to sharing a story, my mouth is usually wide open, but he just tells them like it's another day in the office. And he laughs. They're always funny to him, no matter how ridiculous. But he doesn't talk about why he left…" Crail trails. He looks up at her. "Did he tell you any yet?"

She shakes her head no.

He shrugs. "Just a guy doing a job,' Luke once said."

"What else?" Stella can't help but ask.

"Something about something in Eastern Europe, and then Afghanistan, but…" Charlie wonders to himself. "He doesn't open up too often."

"Oh."

Crail tries to sum it up. "Yeah… Luke… he can laugh and light up a room, or he can walk into one, read every person in it, and just sit quietly to the side. Like last night. He fixes everything or does nothing at all. Hard to put him in any one category."

"Yeah, last night was something else, wasn't it?"

Crail taps the bar with his finger. "You know, that's just it. Intense to us, but normal to him. Maybe that's why…"

"Why what?"

Crail struggles to find the words. "I don't think I've ever met a lonelier guy."

* * *

Luke's truck pulls up to Pierce and Bee's cabin. He walks up to the front stoop, takes a pause, and knocks.

Bee opens it quickly. "Luke! So nice to see you again."

"Hi, Mrs. Bee. Nice to see you too. Is Stella around?"

Saint hears Luke's voice and bounds to the front door. He nearly knocks him over, but Luke holds his own and takes a minute to give Saint all the attention he needs.

Bee represses a wide smile. "She was. She forgot her ID and backtracked to find it. I'm sure she'll be back soon. Won't you come in? Coffee? Late breakfast, or an early lunch?"

"Sure, yes. Thanks."

"What are you guys up to today?" Bee asks casually as they go to the kitchen.

"I, uh, I have flight school. Or flight lessons at least. But I forgot to get her number, and all she told me to do was show up here before noon."

"Ah, well, I'm sure it won't be too long."

She gets him a coffee mug and pushes the coffee pot his way. Luke pours himself a cup and walks around the cabin, then he and Saint step out onto the back deck.

The mountains are beautifully framed, and the sky is bluebird and sunny. He is wondering what the rest of the day is going to bring, when as if on cue, a roaring rumble crosses directly over the cabin.

The Widgeon's silver underbelly and wide wings are unmistakable. It continues in a straight line before turning in a mighty display of power and skill. It lines up with the cabin and slowly descends to the waterline. The plane glances several times before settling down, then throttles slowly up to the dock. The right-side engine turns off first, and the plane idles up to the dock, by which time Luke and Bee have made their way out to meet Stella.

The second engine sputters once and turns off, and Stella pops out of the front nose hatch a moment later. She wears aviators and holds a rope.

"Well, that was impressive," Luke marvels.

Stella tosses him the tie-down rope, and Luke catches it. He pulls and gently brings the plane to the side of the dock before securing it.

"Wanted to make sure everyone was ready," Stella declares. She jumps off the nose and onto the dock. Luke instinctively catches her around the waist.

"Are you here to save me?" she jokes, his hands firmly on her side.

Luke blushes and lets go. "I, uh, didn't want you to fall over."

"I'll remember that for next time."

Bee can't help but laugh. "Well, before you go, I insist you have a quick snack."

They walk to the cabin. Pierce is at the table eating a sandwich. "Thought I heard you fly by," he says as Stella kisses him on the cheek. "And Luke, to what do we owe the pleasure?"

"Flying lessons today, Mr. Pierce."

"First, just *Pierce*. And second, flying lessons? That's one hell of a first date."

Stella smacks her father's shoulder. "Dad, it's not a date. It's a lesson."

Pierce winks at Luke. "Sometimes dates *are* lessons."

* * *

In the cockpit of the Widgeon, Stella and Luke are seated comfortably close to each other. Saint is along for the ride, in the aisle behind them. The dials and controls are vintage, but the important ones have been upgraded over the years. An LCD GPS and newer radio have been added, and the cabin lights have been changed from bulbs to LEDs, but structurally it is the same plane as when it was first manufactured.

Stella gives Luke a headset.

"Can you hear me okay?" she asks, her voice slightly staticky.

"Sure can. How about me?"

"Five by five."

Luke looks back at Saint. "Does he need a headset?"

Stella considers. "No. He's a dog."

"I'm just asking," Luke says. "For the noise."

"I'll make sure to fly quietly," she says sarcastically. "But seriously, he'll be fine. He's been my copilot since he was a puppy."

"Does that make me the new copilot?" he grins.

She shakes her head, smiling. "Yes, sure, if that's what you need. Why not?"

"I've been promoted," Luke brags lightly.

Stella grins and shakes her head again. "All right, repeat after me. Electric and beacon. Prime and pump. Start and throttle. Clear and fly."

"Electric and prime. Start and pump. Throttle… and… and fly?"

"Give me your hand."

He reaches toward her, and she takes his hand. She guides his fingers to each control as she names them. "Electric…"

* * *

Back at the kitchen window, Pierce spies on them with a pair of binoculars. "She's teaching him my technique!" he says to Bee.

Bee looks through the window. "Pierce," she scolds. "She's a grown woman. Quit spying on them."

"But she's teaching *my* technique. That's amazing."

Bee gently pushes the binoculars down and turns his face to her. It is then that he notices she is wearing a nightie.

"Pierce," Bee starts slowly. "We have the whole day to ourselves, and you're choosing to bird-watch."

Pierce nods. "Oh, yes. Great point."

Back outside, one of the Grumman's engines kicks in and starts up. The plane turns away from the dock and, once clear, tests its large flaps. The second engine starts up. The plane gains speed, splashes light sheets of water to the sides, runs for a few more seconds, then takes off into the air.

Pierce watches all of this from the bathroom window.

"Yes! You've got this," he says under his breath.

Bee's voice resonates from the bedroom. "Pierce, I'm not going to tell you again!"

* * *

Stella and Luke fly several thousand feet in the air, seemingly closer to the sides of the mountain ranges than the trees below. Luke is entranced by the lightly snowcapped peaks. The sun glints off the many hidden streams and ponds, some of which have remained nameless and unvisited for hundreds of years.

"It's one thing to see things from the side window in a commercial airplane. It's another thing to see it right in front of you," he says, mesmerized.

Stella smiles and turns the plane toward a valley. "Ready for a landing?"

"So soon? Shouldn't we do a few more laps?"

"So long as there aren't any kayakers in the way, we can do whatever we want," she jokes.

He shakes his head, grinning. "Almost too soon. Almost."

"Let's do some touch-and-goes, then you can take off and land. You up for that?"

"We're really doing this, huh?"

"I'm going to guide you first, trust you second."

Luke adjusts the sun visor and nods. "Fair enough."

"Okay," Stella starts, "First lesson. Aviate, communicate, navigate."

"I should have brought a notebook."

"Repeat it. Aviate, communicate, navigate. Fly the plane, talk on the radio, then get to where you're going."

"Okay, okay. Aviate, communicate… navigate. Fly it, talk it, get there."

Stella chuckles. "Good enough. Now there," she says, pointing at a lake ten miles out. "Aviate us over there."

"What? Like, right now?"

Stella takes her hands off the yoke. "The sooner you start flying, the better."

Luke reaches forward and takes control of the plane. It dips and rises due to his aggressiveness.

"Gentle and confident, not reactive and scared," Stella guides.

Luke looks around to make sure no airplanes or mountains are going to sneak up on them. "Gentle and confident. Yes, ma'am."

* * *

A moose stands up to its knees in one of the many feeder creeks along Lake Koocanusa. It lazily eats roots and only turns its head when the rumble of the Widgeon passes by. The moose observes the loud silver goose touching the water, skimming a few hundred feet, then rising again. After four or five smooth touches, the bird comes back around. The engines flutter, and the plane flies as if scared to commit to the landing. But when it does, it skims, settles heavily, and grumbles.

Inside the cockpit, Stella gives Luke a high five. "That was great!"

"Holy crap, yeah that was!" he says, sweating from the adrenaline.

"All right, so pull out that manual," she instructs.

Luke finds an old binder tucked in a pocket next to his seat. "Okay."

"Now find the section on water takeoff."

He takes a minute and finds it on page 28. "All right, section three, paragraph two, bullet c.: 'Water Takeoff.'"

"Good. Now read it."

"A water takeoff can be made after approximately twenty-five seconds." He pauses. "Wait, that's it? That's all the instruction it gives?"

She grins, "And adjusting the flaps."

He looks out the window at the wings. "How far do we extend them?" he asks.

"Didn't you say you learn by doing?"

He hears the challenge in her voice and puts the manual away, "I think *you* did, but I get it."

Stella looks around and points at the water. "The ripples on the lake indicate the wind is coming straight at us. Left foot, right foot keeps you adjusted. But you want to take off at a slight angle, about twenty degrees." She then taps the airspeed indicator. "This is the ASI, basically the speedometer, but that tells you what she's doing, not what she wants to do." She then takes his hand and puts it on the throttle. "Let me teach you how to feel what she wants. Push these forward till this dial touches here."

She pushes his hand, and the engines respond reliably. They move through the water at below takeoff speeds.

"Then, after about fifteen seconds of this," she continues, "pull back on the yoke and feel if she's ready to lift. It takes a moment to break the water's surface tension, so pull back a little more, and keep it there till we clear the trees. And that's that."

"That's actually a lot," he says, his hands still on the throttle.

"I'll be shadow-handling you," she responds.

The lake is miles long and blue, and the trees sway gently. He looks around and accepts that if others can do it, then maybe so can he. He looks over at his hand and feels the strength in her touch.

"Okay. I'm ready."

"All you, copilot."

"All me." He grins before a wash of seriousness takes hold. Stella watches him transition to all business and focus on the job ahead of him.

"Clear my sectors, and aim into the wind," he says coolly. "Left foot, right foot. Throttle up, speed, pull back, clear trees. Let's do this."

The moose watches the Widgeon throttle up, ride along the water, skip once, and lift off. It flies up and over the lake, then slowly turns away.

Stella lets him fly around a ridge before taking control again. "How 'bout we head back to Flathead for lunch?" she asks.

Luke laughs. "Just like that? Sure, why not."

* * *

The Grumman lands near the bait and tackle shop, and Stella taxis the plane to the dock. She shows Luke the shutdown sequence, then instructs him to secure the plane while she does it. He pops out of the nose and tosses a rope to a dockhand, who secures the plane. Outside, Luke waits for Stella, and when she verifies the plane is properly turned off, she takes the company flight log and credit card, then makes her way to the nose. She also jumps out, but the plane pushes back because the dockhand tied the rope too loose. She stumbles toward the edge of the dock and is about to fall in when Luke catches her by the arm.

They lock eyes, and she feels the strength in his hands.

"I've got you," he says reassuringly.

"Hmm," Stella responds, blushing.

She regains her footing, and Saint comes to the edge of the plane. Luke pulls him out and puts him on the dock.

They get sandwiches and sit at a picnic table overlooking the lake, basking in the sun's warmth while an attendant refuels the Widgeon.

"So, what's the deal with the horse?" Luke asks, indicating the tail.

"My first horse," Stella responds, taking a bite.

He says nothing, and she catches Luke's questioning look.

"Hey," she says, responding to the potential judgment. "My dad started his company with one plane. I flew for him and *earned* my spot as a pilot, and after I worked for a year, I bought a horse. A *rescue* horse, if you care to know. So, if you don't like it, now is probably a good time to start getting over it."

Luke laughs in defense. "I'm sorry."

She looks at him. "You got any more judgy questions?"

Luke's laugh continues. "I said I was sorry! I don't want to get kicked out of flight school on my first day."

Stella gets a message on her phone and checks her watch. "We need to get home soon. Dad has a client to fly. He needs the plane."

Luke gives his sandwich to Saint, who eats it in two bites.

"Can I take off again?" he asks.

She nods. "Okay, but I'll turn it around. Coming off a pier can be tricky."

Luke can't contain his excitement. He practically runs down the dock while Saint bounds after him.

* * *

Pierce paces in the living room. "What if she's late?"

Bee sighs. "She's never been late before. Give her some credit."

"I know, I know, but—"

The Widgeon flies over the house, and the familiar rumble settles Pierce. It carves a long arcing circle and approaches the water. The plane skims but doesn't commit and takes off again. Another arc and another touch, this time fully embracing the landing. The Widgeon putters from a distance off and makes its way to the dock. When it comes near, Luke jumps out and secures the plane.

Pierce greets them.

"Sorry about that," Luke says to him. "We would have been here sooner if I wasn't scared of landing."

"You just gotta hit the ball hard," Pierce offers.

"How's that?"

Pierce thinks for a moment. "Can't hit home runs if you're afraid to swing. Sometimes that's all it takes, just one solid effort."

Stella emerges and jumps onto the dock.

"How'd he do?" Pierce asks.

"Really good."

Pierce nods and looks at them both. "Good instructor and a good student. Great combination. But okay," he says, pointing to Stella's plane, "I've got to take your ride to run a client to Wyoming. I'll be back by morning."

"Just filled her up," Stella smiles, tossing him the keys.

Saint pops his head out, and Luke helps him disembark.

Bee, now out on the dock to see Pierce off, kisses him warmly. "Call me when you get there."

"Don't get into any trouble without me," he replies with a grin.

They wait for Pierce to back-taxi and turn around, then take off expertly. As he does, Luke is wide-eyed with admiration.

"And the way it just takes off, doing what it wants. That plane is amazing."

"It was meant for flying," Stella says assuredly.

Bee leans over to Luke. "So, are you staying for dinner?"

Luke looks over at Stella from the corner of his eye. She has her arms crossed and is watching her father fly away. He says nothing until he notices she shifts her head just a few degrees to hear his response.

He grins. "If it isn't imposing, sure, I would love to."

"No imposition at all. Let's go inside. I'll cook," Bee says happily.

Bee, Luke, and Saint walk back to the cabin, leaving Stella to stay on the dock a moment longer. It is her tradition to watch the plane fly off till it can't be seen anymore.

Back in the cabin, Luke gravitates to the fireplace mantle and picks up a picture he hadn't noticed. A much younger Pierce, with shoulder-length black hair in a leather bomber jacket, stands next to a plane in a desert. Behind him, someone is filling the plane with fuel, and another young guy with a bushy seventies-era mustache stands on the other side of the propeller. They are grinning about something only they would be able to remember.

"Who is this next to Pierce?" Luke asks.

Bee comes over. "That's his cousin. Smartest guy in the world. They flew that plane all over Saudi Arabia and Iran just before everything went political."

"Huh," Luke says, settling into a plush recliner. "Was that before or after the navy?"

"After. He was teaching English overseas. They bought the plane from a stock surplus for a few hundred dollars. Made it to Afghanistan—had to negotiate passage with the mujahideen, then the Soviets—then to India. They cut over, up around the Pacific Rim, and a few months later, got to Alaska. He said they had to refit the engines when he finally made it to Seattle. Then put an ad in the paper and started flying executives and fishermen up and down the West Coast. Bought the little Grumman, and a few years later, he bought the Goose but kept ol' silver. It's been upgraded, Lord I don't know how many times. How'd you like flying it?"

Bee looks over and sees Luke has fallen asleep on the recliner. She smiles and lays a blanket over his feet. Stella comes in midsentence, but Bee shushes her and points to Luke.

"I guess you tuckered him out," Bee whispers with a grin.

"Poor guy." Stella smiles.

* * *

Dusk turns the sky orange-red. Bee reads a book at the dining room table, and Stella comes out of the back room with a laptop in hand, speaking into a headset.

"All right. Tomorrow, Silver Bay," she confirms. "One fuel stop, and we'll have you there by dinner. Sounds great, I look forward to it. Nine in the morning at the docks."

Luke, still in the recliner, grumbles and rubs his eyes.

"Well hello, sleepyhead. How was your nap?" Stella asks.

"Oh man, how long was I out?"

"About an hour and a half."

"Did I snore?"

Bee shakes her head. "Not too bad."

"I'm sorry," he says, running his hand through his hair and stretching. "Then again, that was an amazing nap."

Stella sits on the couch and shrugs. "You needed sleep. You got to sleep."

Luke senses tension. "What is it?"

"I can't find Saint."

"Seriously?"

"Last we saw him was when Dad took off."

"Where've you looked?"

"Around the house. Called some people. No one has seen him."

Luke yawns, stands up, and fishes his truck keys out of his pocket. "Well, let's go drive around."

* * *

Stella sits in the passenger seat, and Luke calls Crail.

"Hey buddy, you seen Saint?" Luke asks.

"No," Crail says. "But I'm at the bar. Let me ask around to see if anyone else has." He turns and addresses the patrons in front of him. "Hey! Has anyone seen a three-legged husky?"

A few people start to laugh, wondering if it is the start of a bad joke.

Crail shakes his head. "I'm serious, anyone seen a white-gray three-legged husky?"

An older lady in the corner raises her hand. "Now that you mention it, I saw a husky about an hour ago, right near Bond Creek, thereabouts, heading… south."

Crail gets on the phone again. "May have been seen near Bond Creek, going south"

"Thanks, man," Luke says. He hangs up and skirts the road, then turns the truck around in one fluid motion. He lets go of the wheel for a quick moment and catches it when it straightens out.

"I think I know exactly where he's going," he says to Stella.

* * *

Thirty minutes later, the truck's headlights splay between trees, and the driveway gives way to reveal Luke's cabin. The headlights show Saint lying on his dog bed, casually looking back at them.

Stella gets out. "There he is!"

Luke nods and turns off the truck. "There he is indeed."

"Saint! What are you doing all the way out here?" she asks.

Saint gives her a lick, then walks over to Luke.

"Whose cabin is this?" she asks.

"Mine. This is where I found him last time, or rather, he found me."

Stella pushes the patio rocking chair. "It's cute."

Luke opens the front door and flicks a light switch. "Thanks. Want me to show you around?"

Stella moves her hair out of her face and smiles. "Yeah."

Inside, the cabin is further along than before. The bed has a very thick and fluffy comforter and multiple blankets. The kitchen sink is installed, and Luke moves a few tools out of the way. The bathroom is almost done being tiled, and Luke lights some kindling in the fireplace.

"It's getting chilly. Need to start a fire to keep the cold at bay."

Stella nods. "You did all this?"

"I did the upgrades. Still need to replace the windows and a few other things. Found that sink at a thrift store. It's completely vintage, and I had to get it."

Stella tests the faucet and feels the water. "Works well."

"And the bathroom needs a lock on the door."

"Better ventilation without one."

"Are you just going to support all my decisions?"

"You're right," she says with a shake of her head. She looks around for something to criticize and points at the floor. "Needs an extra coat of varnish. And that fridge," she says, pointing at the 1940s General Electric, "probably needs a tune-up."

Luke laughs. "That's your full assessment?"

"That's it. You're welcome." She grins.

Saint jumps on the bed.

"Off," Luke says with a snap of his finger.

Saint moans and slides off.

Luke looks back at Stella. "All I have is water and juice. Can I offer you either?"

"Tomorrow is going to be a full day, so Saint and I need to get back."

"Hmm. Yeah, you're right," Luke says.

Stella wonders whether he is going to take no for an answer, but when he finds his keys and smothers the fire, she can't help but feel a hint of disappointment.

"You ready?" he asks, turning to her.

"I am. Let's go."

"Yes, let's. Saint, come on," Luke ushers.

Saint walks out with Luke, and Stella wonders if her dog may have chosen another.

* * *

They drive in silence while Saint sits between them. Luke gently rubs Saint's neck, and after a moment of repressed frustration, Stella finally comes out and says it.

"Are you trying to take my dog?"

"What?" Luke asks, no longer entranced by the simplicity of driving.

"I think you've bribed my dog to like you."

Luke grins and looks over at Saint. "Saint, do you like me?"

Saint looks at him and adjusts his ears but doesn't respond.

"Maybe I have to talk dog," Luke jests. "Saint, *ohwwwww! Ohwwwwwww!*" he howls.

Saint starts to murmur, then howls back ever so quietly.

Luke leans into it and howls longer, "*Ohwwwww-wwwww!*"

Saint joins in unequal harmony.

Stella puts her hands over her face. "You guys are ridiculous."

Saint turns and noses her.

"Tell her to howl too," Luke encourages.

"I do not howl," she exclaims as Saint's cold nose pushes against her neck.

"No one here to judge you but us, and we're already howling. Aren't we, Saint?"

"Oh my God, okay. Okay!" she laughs, pushing Saint out of her face.

They are silent and wait for her to howl.

"*Oww,*" she says conservatively.

Saint looks at Luke, and Luke shakes his head.

"That was more of a word than anything."

Saint grumbles and lets out a very quiet howl. Luke picks it up, then they both turn to Stella. Unable to resist any longer, she belts out her best, and the three of them harmonize for the next few miles.

* * *

The truck pulls up to Stella's home in the deep of the night. She gets out and leaves the door open for Saint. He looks back at her but doesn't exit.

"Saint, c'mon," she calls.

Saint sits and looks back at Luke, and Stella looks at him as well.

"Really?"

Luke puts the truck in park and gets out. He reaches over and scoops Saint to the edge of the door. "Come here, buddy."

Stella watches him lift Saint out and put him down on the ground.

"Oh, now I've seen everything!"

"What? He has a hard time getting in and out," Luke says.

Saint walks over to the house and investigates a plant, and Luke walks up to Stella at the front stoop.

"When can I see you again?" he asks.

"I've got to fly a client and their family to Minnesota tomorrow. So, a few days."

Luke is visibly disappointed. "Who's your copilot?"

She is caught off guard. "I won't have one."

He looks at his feet, then grins. "Well, how am I going to learn to be one if you're not teaching me?"

She crosses her arms. "Really? You want to fly with me tomorrow?"

Luke's eyes gleam. "Absolutely."

She considers this. "Okay. Pack a two-day bag. Be here at eight in the morning. And not a minute late, or I'm leaving without you."

Luke nods. "I'll be early."

She opens the door, and Saint sneaks in. She pauses and looks back. "Okay?"

Luke takes a step closer to her on the stoop. "Okay," he nods.

She walks inside and slowly begins to shut the door behind her.

"Good night," she says with a grin.

Luke waits for the door to shut.

"Good night," he whispers.

He walks back to his truck. Inside, he turns the engine on, finds a song, and is about to put the truck in drive when he smacks the steering wheel.

"I should have kissed her," he says with a shake of his head.

Chapter 6

Luke pulls up to Stella's house early the next morning and sees the Grumman Goose docked at the pier. The plane is a larger version of the Widgeon, with a body painted in vintage tribute and engines that are longer and more forward reaching. He parks the truck out of the way, grabs his weekender bag, then quickly knocks on the front door.

Stella opens it.

"That thing is huge!" he exclaims.

She appreciates his excitement. "Seats eight, the engines are turbocharged, and the bomb bay was replaced with an extended-range fuel tank and cargo hold."

"Bomb bay?"

Stella grins. "Yeah, it used to be a long-range submarine hunter. Designed to hold a two-hundred-fifty-pound bomb and depth charges."

Luke doesn't know what to say but is clearly enamored.

They walk through the cabin, and Saint tries to follow them out the patio doors. Stella pushes him gently back into the house. Luke looks to her for an explanation. "Saint is not coming. Too much liability," she says plainly.

Luke formulates an argument. "We leave him here again, he's liable to run off and never come back."

Stella closes the patio door with simple authority. "Then we'll just get him from your cabin when we get back."

"Touché," Luke says.

Stella walks down the dock to the plane while Saint and Luke look at each other through the glass door.

"Sorry buddy, I tried, but the boss says no," Luke says.

Saint paces uncomfortably. Luke turns and catches up to Stella.

"So, where are we flying to?" he asks.

"Silver Bay."

"Where's that?"

"Lake Superior, close to Canada."

"Who is the client?"

"A media executive and his family, they used to own a lot of Minneapolis radio and TV. Would never guess it though, they're so normal."

Luke and Stella walk up to the Goose and get in through the side door. The cabin is large, the seats are plush, and the cargo area is deep. Luke can't help but whistle.

"All right, cowboy, let's get in and do some preflight checks," Stella guides.

* * *

Back at the cabin, Emily comes to the front door and knocks. She's hand-churned some butter and wants to share.

Bee gets the door. "Emily, how are you?"

"Great! This is for you," Emily says, presenting a mason jar. "And hey, do you have any organic tea or coffee? I need caffeine, but I'm not willing to sacrifice the earth to get it."

Bee laughs and turns to the kitchen. "Sure, come on in. I know Pierce buys some fancy stuff every once in a while. Just got to find it."

Emily enters but doesn't shut the door, and no one notices Saint walk out.

* * *

Back inside the Goose, Stella goes over the plane's features. "Life vests, water, and rations in case something happens. The exit will be out the front or rear, depending on where there's fire. And if there's water within five miles of us, we can pretty much glide there."

She points and instructs Luke to sit down in the copilot seat. She walks him through the preflight checklist, and he complies. Stella then checks her watch. "We've got thirty minutes. You want breakfast? Use the bathroom?"

"Breakfast, yes. Bathroom, maybe." He looks around, contemplating. "This is awesome, by the way. Like a road trip but significantly better."

She absorbs his energy and remembers her first time flying. "I guess it is."

Luke and Stella go to the house, and Stella shares the flight itinerary. "We'll get them from their cabin at nine.

I'll need you to secure the plane to their dock and carry their bags on board. We'll take off and refuel at Lake Sakakawea, which'll be right at our maximum distance. We'll be there for about an hour to refuel, stretch, and eat. Then on to Silver Bay."

Emily greets them as they walk into the cabin. "Morning love bugs! Come here, I need hugs."

Stella and Luke take turns hugging her, then go to the kitchen island. Coffee, scrambled eggs, and toast are spread out. They take bites and pack lunch bags in silence. Luke respects that Stella has transitioned to all business and doesn't tease or get in her way. She reviews the plan with Bee, then kisses her on the cheek.

"Thanks, Mom," Stella says as she gets the lunches.

"Oh, here are my truck keys in case you need to move it. Welcome to use it for anything you want to," Luke says, handing Bee his keychain.

Bee nods and appreciates his thoughtfulness, "Thank you. And okay, last check. Pilots are good? Well rested? Ready to go?" she asks.

"Pilots?" Emily asks with a widening smile. She puts an arm around Luke's shoulder. "Luke, if this match isn't made in the cosmos, then I don't know what to make of it."

Luke chuckles. "Still learning. Got a long way to go."

Stella looks around. "Have you seen Saint?"

Bee furrows her brow. "I saw him this morning."

Luke points at the open front door. "I'm going to assume he went that way."

Stella is concerned, but Bee gets ahead of it. "Saint will be fine, and he'll be here when you get back." She checks her watch. "Besides, the two of you need to get going."

Luke pours coffee in a thermos but sees that Stella is not convinced. "I'll call Crail and have him check on my cabin in case he shows up there," he assures.

"Okay," Stella concedes. She then turns to Bee. "Dad gets in later?"

Bee nods. "Yes, he already called. This afternoon."

"All right, we're going. Love you," she says with a hug.

Bee reciprocates and ushers them out. Emily waves, and Luke and Stella make their way down the dock to the Goose. Luke unties the plane and gently pushes it away from the dock, then closes the side door. Stella is in the cockpit and starts flipping switches. She revs up the number one engine and, once it is running smoothly, preps the number two, at which point Luke has already sat down and put his headset on.

"Ready?" Stella asks him.

"Absolutely."

She takes his hand and guides him in turning on the number two engine, and after a second, the engine fires up and they take off. Through it all, no one notices Saint hiding under the tarp in the rear cargo hold.

They are in the air for less than two minutes before descending and taxiing to an enormous, lodge-like cabin. Several boaters and excited kids wave at them as the Goose motors by. Luke is more than happy to wave back, and Stella guides the plane to the dock where a family and a set of bags await. The kids cover their ears, and a porter stands next to the luggage.

Stella comes over the headset and speaks to Luke. "Poke your head out the back. Make sure we don't hit the dock."

"On it!" Luke says, quickly unbuckling. He pops the door and prepares a line. The engine throttles down throatily, and the plane docks safely. Luke works with the porter and starts loading bags while Stella exits and meets the Cohls. She shakes hands and gives a quick update, then ushers the family on board for a safety brief. It's a full flight with Mr. and Mrs. Cohl and their three kids. Stella introduces Luke while he closes the back door.

"And this is Michael, Ryan, and Anna," Mr. Cohl says, pointing at the kids.

Luke shakes their hands as he walks past, then sits down and dons his headset.

"Ready?" Stella asks as she checks gauges.

"Always ready." He grins.

The plane chokes and throttles, and they are in the air less than a minute later.

*　*　*

A few hours later, having flown east over the entirety of Montana, they prepare to land in North Dakota. The weather is less favorable, and the clouds are lower. Stella guides the plane under the cloud deck, and they abort the first landing because a sailboat is too close. They land on the second pass, and Luke unbuckles to take his customary position as dockhand. They dock, Stella shuts down the plane, and Luke secures it. He eagerly helps the kids and Mr. and Mrs. Cohl out. Stella watches him do this, and despite not understanding the full gravity of his boyish smile, she feels her heart swell a little in her chest.

Once everyone is out, Stella and Luke follow, and she prepays for fuel.

"Burgers and bathroom?" she asks.

Luke laughs. "Absolutely."

Saint figures this is also a good time for a bathroom break, and he climbs out from the cargo hold and down the ladder. He trots down the dock, finds a tree, and looks over at Luke, who has just seen him.

"Uh oh," Luke says quietly, gently nudging Stella with his elbow. "We have a problem."

"What's that?" Stella asks, following his gaze and seeing Saint.

"Oh, well there's that."

"What do we do?" Luke whispers. "We can't leave him here."

Stella considers their options. After a moment, she walks up to Mr. Cohl. "Sir, I think we have a stowaway."

She points at Saint and explains the situation.

Mr. Cohl takes it in, then politely waves Luke over.

"So, we have a stowaway?" he asks them.

Luke nods. "Yes sir, must have snuck in when we were… well, don't know when…. he just did."

Mr. Cohl and the three of them look over at Saint, who is now on his back being rubbed by the older kid, Michael.

"He sure did." Mr. Cohl nods, "And I'd ask if he's good with kids, but clearly is."

"He'll be quiet as a mouse, I swear," Stella reassures.

"It's okay. The kids have been bugging me for a dog for a while, and this might buy me some time." Mr. Cohl laughs. "But he was really on our flight the whole time?"

Stella raises her eyebrows and nods. "Yup. In the back. Never saw him."

"Well, we can't leave him here, and I don't reckon we can turn around. How much farther to Silver Bay?"

"Another three hours."

"Oh, that's all? It's fine. Absolutely."

"Thank you so much, and I'm sorry for any inconvenience or dog hair!" Stella exhales.

Mr. Cohl tries to calm her apprehension. "We've been flying with your dad for years. This is nothing. Did he ever tell you about the time we had to fly out of the way of a tornado?"

"What? No, he didn't!"

He chuckles. "So, you see, a stowaway dog is no issue at all."

They share a good-natured laugh and finish lunch while the kids play tag with Saint on the beach. Soon, the plane is repacked, refueled, and back in the air.

Luke turns to see Michael lying on the floor against Saint's side. He is reading a book out loud, and Saint is sleeping.

Luke turns back to Stella, "You did good."

"*We* did good."

He nods. "Fact."

* * *

The sun is setting when the Goose lands on Lake Superior. It taxis to the Silver Bay Marina and is tied off. Everyone disembarks, and the Cohls' bags are carried to an awaiting car.

Mr. Cohl turns to Stella and Luke. "Where are you guys staying tonight?"

"The motel downtown, but I don't know if they take dogs."

"Nonsense. We have a guest house. You're welcome to stay. Saint, too, of course."

"Are you sure?" Stella asks.

Mr. Cohl waves at the driver and asks him to bring another car. "Absolutely. Think nothing of it."

Luke helps Stella lock up the plane, and they load into the second car with Saint. They drive away along the darkening lakefront and pull off the main road a short distance later. Trees obscure the house from the road, but the closer they get, the more they see of the sprawling Victorian home. It is light gray, three stories tall, and has multiple wings with large windows. The Cohls' car goes to the main house, and Stella, Luke, and Saint turn onto a secondary driveway. They park in front of a fairytale-style cottage, complete with a pond and back porch.

"This is beautiful," Stella whispers.

"This is a guest house?" Luke asks as they enter the foyer.

Stella grins. "I know, right?"

He walks through the living room and exits out the side to a large patio. A fire pit sits in the middle and overlooks the pond. Saint runs to the water and a family of frogs stops croaking.

"Want to make a fire later?" Luke asks.

"That would be great."

There's a knock on the front door, and Saint barks an alert.

Stella opens it to reveal Mr. Cohl with a kid sitting on his shoulders.

"Better than the motel downtown, I hope?"

Stella nods vigorously. "Amazing! Thank you so much."

Luke is out by the fire pit, splitting wood.

Mr. Cohl looks around. "My pleasure. It was meant for my mother-in-law, but she passed away before she could see it."

"Oh, I'm so sorry."

"Thank you. So, no food in the fridge since we've been gone for a few weeks. We're putting a big grocery order in. I'll have one of the kids run down here, and you guys make a list of anything you want for tonight, for breakfast, and for the trip back tomorrow. Whatever you need. Really."

"Are you sure?"

Mr. Cohl laughs. "Well, your dad didn't tell you the tornado story. Did he at least tell you about the time an engine blew and we camped on an island for two days till someone could get us?"

"What!" Stella exclaims.

Mr. Cohl chuckles. "Exactly. So, food and a place to stay are the least I can offer you and your boyfriend."

Stella blushes. "He's not my boyfriend."

Mr. Cohl winks. "Right. I won't tell Pierce."

"I'm serious!"

He laughs heartily and looks up at his kid. "We didn't see anything, did we?"

The little boy shakes his head. "Nothing!"

Mr. Cohl leaves with a chuckle, and Stella closes the door. Luke comes in a moment later.

"Everything all right?"

"They're getting groceries for us. We literally don't have anything to do till tomorrow morning."

Luke looks at her for a long while. She is about to ask him something to break the intensity when he leans forward and kisses her deeply. He holds her close for a moment before pulling away, and her eyes stay closed.

"Today was amazing," he finally says.

Stella's eyes flutter as she tries to keep her composure. "I, um, yes. It was. And that kiss…"

"Can I do it again?"

"Please," she says quickly, leaning in for another.

He draws her close and kisses her again, sliding his hands down her back. Time passes with ultimate slowness and all sounds disappear.

"So," he says after a moment. "What's the plan?"

Stella takes a breath and puts a hand on his chest to create a little space between them. She sees a Scrabble board on the coffee table.

"Scrabble?"

Luke grins. "Careful what you ask for. I'm a jack-of-all-trades."

"Is that so?" she says, trying to shift her mind from what she really wants to do.

They set up the board and look at each other with mutual admiration.

Stella goes first. Her opening word is *farts*.

Luke laughs out loud, then counters with *tiger*.

Stella's competitive streak is activated. "Tiger? Here I am playing at a first-grade level, trying to take it easy on you."

Luke grins, and she can't help but be distracted.

Stella continues, "I'm going to have to do better than *farts* if this is going to go anywhere."

"What's *what* going where, exactly?" Luke asks, implying a deeper meaning.

"I'm… uh… you know."

"Stella," Luke says, being very forward with her. "Can I be very honest?"

She looks at him but isn't sure she is ready to hear what he is about to say.

"No more games," he says calmly.

She fiddles with a letter square. "Other than Scrabble? I'm sure there are others. Maybe backgammon?" she deflects, looking under the coffee table.

He takes her hand in his and holds her gaze. "I mean us."

She looks at him. "I'm not playing games with you, if that's what you're asking."

He is calm. "That is what I'm asking. I mean, Mr. Cohl basically thinks I'm your boyfriend."

"You were eavesdropping!"

He grins. "For what it's worth, I like you. A lot."

Stella sighs and puts *jade* on the board. "I like you a lot too."

Luke evaluates the words in front of him and takes a few more letters from the pile. "Well, if you're okay with it, I'd like to finish this game, have dinner, then maybe figure it out from there."

There is a pause, he looks at the board, then puts a *d* at the end of *jade*.

She quickly counters with an s at the end of *tiger*.

"So long as you're not a sore loser," Stella says, grinning widely.

* * *

Food arrives in several grocery bags, and Stella tells Luke to take a shower while she cooks. He finishes and steps out from behind the curtain. The mirror is steamed, and he wraps himself with a white towel. He brushes his teeth and puts on deodorant, then walks into the bedroom where he puts on jeans and a T-shirt. He stays barefoot and steps into the hall to see Stella in the kitchen. She wears a single long braid and dances to old-school blues while searing steaks in the oven. Two glasses of red wine are on the counter, and she turns to work on a caprese salad. She takes a bite of mozzarella, then looks up to see Luke leaning against the wall.

"And how long have you been standing there?" she asks.

"Long enough."

She picks up the wine and walks over to him. He takes it, then reaches for the cheese in her hand. He nibbles it, and she kisses him.

"Really good," he compliments.

She takes a sip. "Wine is pretty good too."

"What are we celebrating?"

She thinks for a moment. "Your first real flight."

"Absolutely. Cheers to that."

"And us," she adds.

"Oh?" he grins.

Stella shakes her head. "That's too much. I'm sorry."

"I'm not saying it is. I'm just asking… you know, what we might be."

She studies him and can't help but touch his chest. "Is there any hot water left?"

"Probably."

"Watch the steaks. I like mine medium rare."

Luke nods and watches her go. "Yes, ma'am."

* * *

Luke sits calmly by the outdoor fire pit on a lounge chair. It is dark, and his face is lit in the flickering glow of orange and yellow. He holds his glass of wine, with Stella's on the side table. Saint is lying on the ground next to him. From the side, he sees Stella walk barefoot into the kitchen. She is in a yellow sundress, and her hair is loose. She samples another bite of cheese, then walks out onto the back patio.

"Well, hello," Luke says.

She approaches him with a saunter, then moves her hair out of the way.

"May I sit?" she asks.

"Of course," he responds, pulling another lounge chair over to him.

She takes a sip of her wine and puts it down, then does the same with his. She straddles his lounger and sits on his lap, all without taking her eyes off him. He instinctively sits more upright and reaches forward, pulls her toward him, inhales deeply, and kisses her, then her neck.

She exhales softly and runs her fingers through his hair. Not one to rush nor shy away, he lifts the edges of her dress and moves his hands behind her. His fingertips trail along soft skin, and he caresses the top of her hips and lower back, exploring with gentle respect. She pushes his hands down until they rest on the tops of her thighs, and they stop to look at each other with adult understanding.

"Is this okay?" he asks in an undeniable display of patient desire.

She takes his face in her hands. "More," she whispers.

Luke stands up with her around his hips. He secures her legs around him. "What about this?"

She grins and kisses him. "More."

He carries her to the kitchen. "I made dinner. How's that?"

"Well, I'm still starving," she says. "But right now, I'm very distracted."

He moves to the kitchen island and uncovers the steaks. Stella, with her legs still wrapped around him, reaches over, cuts a piece, and feeds it to him. She then cuts another and takes a bite.

"Oh, my lord, that's good," she compliments before tossing a piece to Saint.

Luke takes another bite. "Napkin, please."

Stella dabs his mouth, then returns to kissing him.

A quick bite of salad and refilled wine later, he carries her to the bedroom. Saint follows, but the door shuts before he can make it into the room. He is momentarily unhappy, whines, then remembers the steaks. He heads to the kitchen, licks the remnants of steak juices off the floor, and sniffs around the top of the counter. He is unable to reach the plates, so he goes outside and curls up on the lounger Luke had been sitting on.

He watches the fire pit flicker its last fingerlings of flame and goes to sleep.

Chapter 7

Saint barks.

Luke and Stella are asleep on a king-sized bed. The blanket is thick and barely covers her, and nearly every pillow is on the floor. The light from the moon cuts through a slit in the window panels and caresses Luke's back.

Saint barks again.

Luke stirs and Stella moves her arm. He pushes the blanket over and gets out of bed, then rubs his shoulder and makes sure the sheets still cover Stella's body. When Saint barks one more time, Luke is in the middle of using the bathroom. After he flushes, Saint's toenails rapidly click on the kitchen floor, this time accompanied by a faint whimper.

"Oh, all right, buddy. You can come in," Luke whispers as he opens the door.

Saint stands in the opening but doesn't come in. He is clearly agitated.

"C'mon, you weren't kicked out for that long," Luke consoles.

Saint barks loudly and runs outside. He stops in the living room and looks back to see if Luke has followed him.

He has not.

Saint runs back to the room and, seeing Luke back under the sheets, barks loud enough to wake Stella.

"Saint, *shhh*," she mumbles.

Luke is now concerned. He wants to fall back asleep, but a nagging doubt starts to grow. He stands up, puts on a pair of jeans, and follows Saint out into the living room. Saint barks louder and moves to the patio. Luke meets him outside, and the early fall air brushes against his back and causes him to shiver.

"What? A bear? A moose?"

Saint barks at the forest, and Luke steps next to him. All is silent, and no animal is about, but then Luke sees a dull-orange bulbed light farther back in the trees. He looks closer and wonders if a hiker or boater has gotten lost, and tiredly watches the flashlight move this way and that but not get closer. Luke is generally underconcerned and wonders if the cottage has a coffee machine. He considers going back in and yawns with a big stretch. Then, after moving his head just a few inches to the side, he recognizes the flashlight to be a flicker of flame.

The familiar rush of adrenaline floods his body, and he is instantly awake. He takes a few steps to the side and, through a clearing between the dark trees, sees that the flame is dancing along the roofline of the Cohls' house.

"Oh shit!"

He rushes back into the cottage and shakes Stella awake. "Fire! Wake up! Call the fire department!"

"What?" she stirs with confusion.

Luke grabs his shoes and slips them on. "The Cohls' house is on fire! I'll get them out. You get the fire department here! Go!"

She throws the blanket to the side. "On it!" she shouts.

Luke and Saint run through the forest up the hill to the Cohls' home. By the time they reach the front door, the fire is spreading from the chimney and illuminating the side of the house with a menacing dance.

Luke bangs on the front door and rings the doorbell in rapid succession while Saint barks in added alarm.

"Mr. Cohl! Your house is on fire! Get up! Get out!" he shouts.

No one answers, and not one to wait around, Luke takes a step back and kicks the door. It takes two solid heel strikes before the lock splinters, and he charges through without delay.

"House is on fire! Get out!" Luke shouts into the open darkness. He reaches for the light switches and flicks them on and off, but the power is already out.

A confused Mr. Cohl, with baseball bat in hand, comes out of a side room. "Where? In the cottage?"

"No! Here! By the chimney!" Luke says sternly. "Everyone out! Stella is calling the fire department."

Mr. Cohl rubs his head. "But the fire alarms haven't gone off—" The upstairs fire alarms start bleating.

"Quick, where are the kids?" Luke asks.

"They're all upstairs."

Luke and Mr. Cohl bound up. When they reach the second floor, a thin layer of light gray smoke is already clouding the ceiling. They crouch down at the landing.

"Where are they?" Luke asks.

"One this way, the other two that way."

"I'll get the two, you get the one."

Luke crawl-rushes down the hall and opens the first door. Saint bumps past him and pokes his nose into a small closet. They head to the next doorway, and Luke opens it and sees kid toys and posters. He rushes to the bed, and Saint runs up with him. Luke sees the outline of a small body under the sheets and scoops it up. He wraps the child in a blanket, and they start and wrestle.

Luke is deliberate but firm. "House is on fire, you're going to be okay, time to go."

The kid whimpers some, and when Luke exits the room, the smoke is darker and lower. Luke takes a deep breath, leans down, and protectively cradles the kid. The smoke is starting to grow thick, and by the time he reaches the landing, he is shuffling on hands and knees.

Mr. Cohl hands the child to Mrs. Cohl, who has met them at the stairs.

"Where's the last kid?" Luke asks.

"Michael, last room!" Mr. Cohl points. He then starts to crawl past him down the hall, but Luke grabs him by the ankle and pulls him back.

"I'll go. You wait here," Luke instructs.

"But it's my son!" Mr. Cohl exclaims.

A flash of flame dances along a billow of smoke, and the two men feel the thousand-degree heat against their skin.

"Then I'm their best chance," Luke says sternly. He doesn't mention that he has rationalized the death of a father as being worse for the family than the loss of a random copilot.

Mr. Cohl kicks Luke's hand away and starts crawling, but he is immediately pulled back by the strength of a man who is no longer taking no for an answer.

The two men share a stern look.

"Take Saint," Luke instructs. "I'll get Michael. You go outside and coordinate the firetruck."

Mr. Cohl knows they're wasting precious time and stubbornly nods. He takes Saint's collar and takes a few steps down the stairs where the air is clearer. "I'll be waiting right here."

Luke starts crawling down the hall, and Saint starts to squirm. Mr. Cohl tries to lead Saint down the stairs, but in a quick flick, Saint breaks his collar and sprints up after Luke.

Mrs. Cohl comes up to her husband. "Ryan and Anna are outside with Stella," she says between smoke-induced coughs.

"Get me the fire extinguisher from the kitchen, then wait outside with the kids. Okay?" Mr. Cohl says. He then quickly kisses her. "I love you."

"Oh God, this isn't happening. This isn't happening!" Mrs. Cohl repeats as she rushes down the stairs.

At the near end of the hallway, Luke can feel the heat against his back. It radiates through the dark smoke and is only a few degrees away from lighting. He finds the last door and reaches up through the smoke to grab the doorknob. It burns his palm, and he curses quickly. He spits in his hand and grabs the knob again. It sizzles, but Luke is able to open the door. Saint leaps over him, and they both rush in. Luke shuts the door behind them, and they stand in the smokeless room.

He looks at Saint. "You're as stubborn as I am!"

Saint barks and they run to the bed. It is empty. Luke looks under the mattress, but Michael isn't under there either. He slaps the frame and, in a moment of anger, flips the bed to ensure no what-ifs if things turned out for the worse and Michael had indeed been hiding under it. But nothing is under it other than a few boxes of clothes and toys.

"Michael! Where are you!" Luke shouts. "There's a fire! We've got to go!"

He looks around the room and sees another door, which is a bathroom. He checks behind the door and shower curtain, but it is empty.

Luke comes back to the bedroom and makes a tactical decision. "Saint, no one is here. Maybe he already got out—time to go!"

Saint barks and scratches at another door. Luke opens it to see Michael curled up in the corner of a large closet, terrified, holding a stuffed animal.

"Good find," Luke says to Saint. He turns his attention to Michael and pulls him out none too gently. "The house is on fire, we've got to go, we're going to be fine, okay?"

"Okay," Michael stammers.

Luke finds a blanket and wraps him up. He picks up the bundle and goes to the door. The doorknob is hotter than before, and smoke seeps in from the top of the frame. Luke shakes his head and doesn't like what he is about to encounter.

"Ready?" he asks the bundle.

Michael mumbles compliance.

"Ready?" Luke asks Saint.

Saint barks and growls at the door.

Luke opens it and is greeted by a punchy wall of black smoke. It sears his arm, and Luke drops to the ground. The extra oxygen from the room combines with the smoke, and a flame, once hidden near the landing of the stairs, shows its true intention. It flares angrily, and Mr. Cohl, who has been committed to his position, blasts the fire extinguisher up at it. The effort is not enough, and Luke barely has time to shout, "Got Michael! We're good!" before a billow of flame rushes down the hall to consume him.

Luke slams the door, and the backdraft rattles against the other side. Despite the door only being opened for a few seconds, the room chokes with smoke. Luke crawls across the floor to the other wall and puts his bundle under the windowsill. He goes back to the bathroom and quickly evaluates the sink, toilet, and shower. He takes several towels and throws them into the middle of the bathroom, then opens the cabinet under the sink and rips out the water pipes so they pour freely. He removes the lid from the toilet bowl and uses it to break the side of the tank, then turns the showerhead, aims it out of the tub, and turns it on full. The towels on the floor soak up water and are sopping wet a few moments later. He scoops them up, runs to the bedroom, and tosses a towel over Michael, then places the other towels against the base of the bedroom door. Only then does he return to the bedroom window to open it. The burst of fresh air is invigorating, and he pushes the screen out with a flat-handed slap.

He sticks his head out and sees red and blue emergency lights flashing in the distance. He then looks back at the bedroom door to see that it is glowing. There is no way the firetrucks will reach them in time, and he shuts the bedroom window.

"All right," he says to Michael and Saint, "It's time for all of us to get to the bathroom."

Michael gets up and shuffles quickly, but Saint stays in the bedroom. His hackles are arched, and he growls at the door. Luke, meanwhile, rips the curtains off the curtain rods and pulls the sheets off the bed. He checks the closet and finds a few more blankets, then rushes with them into the bathroom. He is about to shut the bathroom door when he sees Saint still in the bedroom.

"Saint! Get in here!"

Saint refuses, and Luke looks at the linens in his hands. He tosses the sheets on the countertop and drops a blanket on the wet floor, then runs back into the bedroom. He reaches for the collar and, not finding it, hooks Saint by the neck to pull him back. Saint barks ferociously, making it clear his intent to stay, but Luke is having none of it.

"We don't have time for this!" he shouts and tries to scoop him up.

Saint wriggles out of the hold and commits to his position.

Not to be outdone, Luke grabs him by the tail and pulls him into the bathroom. Saint tries to charge back into the bedroom, but Luke stands in front of the door and wraps a hand over Saint's snout to get his attention.

They look each other in the eyes.

"Stay!" Luke growls firmly.

Saint snarls tremendously but doesn't rush past, and Luke grabs the wet blanket off the floor. He drapes it over the door, then shuts it as hard as he can to create an airtight seal. He places the remaining towels against the bottom of the door and takes solace in seeing the floor is flooded with a quarter inch of water.

He hopes his improvisation has bought them enough time and goes to the bathroom window. It is smaller than the bedroom window but large enough to squeeze through. He opens it fully. The air is crisp and clean, and he starts to tie the ends of the sheets together. When he has tied several, he hangs them out of the window to see if they'll reach the ground. In doing so, he sees Stella standing near the front of the house and shouts for her.

"Stella!"

She hears him first, then sees him, and runs to the side of the house. "Luke!"

"We're okay!" he shouts. "But we're stuck in the bathroom. I'm going to lower them down!"

"Okay! Hurry up! The fire is spreading!"

Luke gets back into the bathroom and makes a loop with another sheet. It is their last and will have to do.

Michael watches him silently, and Luke kneels in front of him.

"All right," Luke instructs. "This goes over your head and under your arms. If you keep your elbows down, it stays locked. If you raise them, you'll slip out. So, stay locked till you get close to the ground," he coaches. "Don't grab at anything either. I'll lower you the whole way. Deal?"

Michael nods quietly, and Luke loops the sheet under his armpits. He tests the system by pulling him a few inches off the floor, then retests the knots holding the improvised rope together. Content but not happy, he ties an anchor knot at the end of the tail and tucks it under his arm.

"All right, get out of the window. I've got you the rest of the way," Luke says.

Michael doesn't move, and Luke becomes keenly aware of smoke entering the room through the vent above. Sensing his hesitation, Luke picks Michael up and lifts him to the window.

"All right, kiddo. Lock your arms."

Michael does so but doesn't want to go out, so Luke pushes him. There is a slight drop, the curtain knots hold, and after twenty quick feet, Stella and Mr. Cohl receive him. Mr. Cohl gives Michael an all-embracing hug, then sends him to Mrs. Cohl who has corralled the kids along the driveway.

"Now you!" Stella demands, shouting back to Luke.

"I have to get Saint out!"

"What? Why is he even with you?" she exclaims. "Get out already!"

"I have to get him out!" Luke shouts down to her.

"He'll jump when you're safe! Please Luke! Just get out!" she shouts frantically.

Luke looks back in the bathroom. Saint is growling and his paws splash water as he snarls at the vent above. The plastic is starting to drip, and an orange finger works out of the sides. The vent's edges peel as a red hand enters the bathroom. It searches for oxygen, and finding some, shoves an arm through looking for more.

Saint jumps to bite it.

"Saint, let's go, you're next!" Luke shouts from the window.

Saint is no longer paying attention to Luke. Seeing this, Luke grabs him. This time, however, Saint nips at Luke's hand. Angry at the blood on his palm but understanding Saint's reasoning, Luke grabs Saint full-bellied and lifts him up off the floor.

Saint fights to get free, and Luke slips on the wet floor. He hits the side of his head against the tub, groans, and passes out. The Fire Demon sees Luke lying facedown in the water, grins, and tries to enter the bathroom.

* * *

Luke spits water and comes to.

A dribble of blood works down the side of his head and falls in several thick drops. He picks himself up off the floor, and the pain in his shoulder causes him to grimace. It is visibly dislocated, and he cradles it.

"Saint, you son of a bitch." He groans.

Undeterred, Luke reaches for him again, but Saint intentionally steps away. Thick black smoke and dashes of flame are now entering the bathroom, and Saint warns the Fire Demon to stay away with another vicious bark.

Luke sees the neck of the toilet seat and crawls to it. He reaches up and gets the sheets, then he reaches up and gets the sheets, then ties the end around the base of the toilet in a loop around the base. He looks up at the window above him, and it billows smoke. He then sees that the bedroom door has started to leak smoke as well, and the top of the door frame is crackling black. The water pipes have also stopped spewing water, and the shower dribbles weakly.

He looks back to Saint and shakes his head. "Saint, I mean it, man. Last chance."

Saint turns his attention to the other door and barks relentlessly. But then he looks back and sees Luke, runs to him, licks his hand, and returns to the fight.

Luke nods, wipes a tear, and pulls the slack out of the sheets. He takes a deep breath, and with a quick heave, climbs up to the billowing window. He considers giving one last test on the knots just to make sure they're secure, then pauses and wonders if he could scoop Saint in a large wrap.

Maybe he'll jump to me if I yell for him?

Luke straddles the window, one leg on each side. He tries to call Saint's name, but the smoke is too thick, and he can't even open his mouth.

Outside, the volunteer firemen have unfurled their hoses and have started spraying the front of the house. An ambulance is working up the driveway as well, but inside, the Fire Demon cares for none of it. It has lingered in the dark smoke for just this moment. Sensing Luke's distraction, it rushes along the ceiling toward the window. It pauses for just a moment when it is directly above him.

Now or never.

The Demon lunges—its fiery hand rushes at Luke's shoulder.

From the wall of smoke, Saint jumps up and bites the Fire Demon by the wrist. Luke feels Saint's fur brush against his leg. He reaches out for him but loses his balance.

He falls out the bathroom window.

Air.

He desperately grabs at anything and, after a moment of nothingness, feels the bedsheets rushing past his fingertips. He feels the first knot go past his legs, and he instinctively wraps his thighs as if he had been fast-roping out of a helicopter. Sensing time slow down, he grabs tighter. The friction burns his fingertips, but it is enough to slow his fall, and when the last knot passes through his hands, he hits the ground with an audible grunt.

Stella and Mr. Cohl rush up to him.

Luke is on his back, covered in dark soot, and Stella pats him down to make sure he is in one piece.

"Oh my God, are you okay? Are you okay?" she asks rapidly.

"Arm hurts. I think it's dislocated," Luke says quietly, opening his watery eyes.

Mr. Cohl looks at his shoulder and nods. "Doesn't look good."

Luke lifts his wrist out to him. "Hold, pull firmly, then move my wrist across my front. I'm not going to be happy, but I need you to do it before I change my mind."

Mr. Cohl does so and resets the shoulder with a pop and a grimace.

A firefighter rushes over to check on them, and in a coherent moment, Luke grabs him. "Spray all the water you can into that window! My dog is in there!"

The firefighter looks at the window Luke is pointing at. The billowing smoke is black, and the tail end of the sheet falls from the windowsill like a discarded cigarette. Luke sees it but refuses to accept what it means.

"Water, that window! Now!"

The firefighter nods. "I'll do what I can."

Small embers float around them and fade to char, and Stella smothers Luke in kisses. "You heroic bastard. Never do that again. Ever. Okay?"

Luke shakes his head. "All right, all right."

Just then, high above them, a corner of siding, its nails having melted, gives way in a slow groan. A twenty-foot-long sheet of the house pendulums toward them.

The Firefighter sees this. "Get back!" he shouts.

Luke grabs at Stella, but he is not fast enough. A piece of the house swings down, hits her in the temple, and the fire roars in satisfaction. Stella crumples to the ground, and Luke struggles to protect her from falling embers.

"We have to get out of here!" Luke shouts.

He braces Stella by her lower back and secures the nape of her neck as best he can while Mr. Cohl carries her legs. The Firefighter rushes back to them and helps them along as more parts of the house fall. From the front of the house, the Firefighters turn their hoses and spray a protective mist over them.

"She got hit in the head! I need a neck and back brace," Luke shouts as they get to the ambulance.

He lays Stella down in the grass, and a younger firefighter, his hair curly red, runs up. He carries a backboard and positions it next to them. He, Luke, and Mr. Cohl secure Stella and emplace the neck brace. They throw open the back of the ambulance and load her onto the gurney.

The Fire Marshal, an older man, comes over and has a quick conversation with the Medic. Luke recognizes the skepticism in their conversation and cuts between them. She is still unconscious, and he checks Stella's wrist for a pulse. Not finding one, he checks her neck. The pulse is weak and thready, and he takes the Medic's penlight to check her pupils — one is large and unreactive, the other is pinpoint.

"Urgent surgical," Luke says to himself. He then turns to the Medic. "She needs an emergency room. Where's the nearest hospital for head trauma?"

"We have a little clinic in town. Will have to call and wake the doc."

"Not a *clinic* doc. A neurosurgeon," Luke stresses.

"Minneapolis," the Medic says.

"It's a three-and-a-half-hour drive," the Fire Marshal adds somberly.

The Medic nods and moves to the ambulance. "We'll drive as fast as we can."

"Can we get a police escort?" Mr. Cohl asks. "Or flight for life?"

The Fire Marshal considers this. "The airport doesn't have night lights. So, they'll send a helicopter."

"How long?" Luke asks.

"Maybe two and a half hours. Round trip."

Luke looks down at Stella and sees her shallow breathing. Her chest stops moving, and his heart falls to the bottom of the earth. She then starts breathing again, but more rapidly.

"We don't *have* three hours."

There is a moment of painful consideration, and all but Luke are prepared to accept it.

"The plane," he says.

"The airport... it can't take a plane at night," the Marshal reiterates.

"No, not *an* airplane," Luke says quickly. "*Her* plane. The air boat!"

* * *

The ambulance pulls up to the dock as the sky gives way to morning. The back doors open, and the Medic and Mr. Cohl wheel Stella out on a gurney. Luke runs down the dock and opens the side door to the Goose. He turns on the lights, sits in the pilot seat, and rummages for the manual. Finding it, he throws on the headset while watching the gurney come down the dock. He wants to make sure she's okay but shakes his head and thumbs to the "Startup" section of the manual.

"Okay, first thing's first. What's the first thing? Focus, focus, focus," he repeats to himself. He then takes a deep breath, closes his eyes, calms himself, and reengages. He scans the manual and accordingly flicks switches, checks gauges, confirms indicators, and turns nobs.

"The gurney won't fit!" the Medic yells from outside the plane.

"Then take her off it and strap her to the floor!" Luke shouts back, trying to stay focused. He turns on the ignition for one engine and hears the pistons move into compression. He is momentarily frozen and realizes he has no idea what to do if they don't start, but they give way and start firing. He smacks the dash in satisfaction and appreciates the plane's willingness to work with him despite the cold and abrupt handling.

He looks back and sees the struggle to board Stella and rushes back to help. She is on the backboard, and he lifts her through while grunting through the pain in his shoulder. The Firefighter that helped him strap Stella is also aboard, and Luke quickly shuts the side door.

"Make sure the board is secured tight!" he says while pulling the waist buckles down to the floor and wrapping them through the backboard's handholds. "I'm going to take off in one minute or less!"

Luke rushes back to the cockpit and turns the throttle up on the running engine. He shifts the tail rudders just like he had seen Stella do the day before, and the plane turns from the marina. But just as it has pulled a few feet away, a front dock rope, which hadn't been released from the nose, pulls them violently back to the side. The plane's right front quarter panel slams into the dock with an audible crunch, and metal scrapes against concrete.

"Ah, dammit!" Luke curses.

Mr. Cohl sees this, runs down the dock, and ducks under the wing. He unfastens the rope and pushes the plane away with a seated kick, and Luke gives him a quick wave. Sensing that they should be clear, he starts the second engine, and it kicks up on the first crank.

With no time to spare, Luke drives the plane past boats and spreads a tall wake. He quickly remembers Stella's first lesson.

"Aviate, communicate, navigate."

He looks back at Stella, then at the Firefighter. "You ready?"

The Firefighter nods. "Ready."

Luke checks his seatbelt, looks ahead, sees clear water, and pushes the throttles forward. The turbos kick in, and the plane gains speed with ease. The windshield is sprayed with water, and he counts out loud. When he reaches fifteen, he pulls firmly back on the yoke and holds it there.

The belly makes one final cut before lifting with smooth intention, and Luke's eyes narrow as the world opens before him.

The sun pokes over the horizon, and he realizes he doesn't know where to go. "Which way is Minneapolis? South? South, right?" he asks.

The Firefighter looks out the side window. "That way," he points. "Keep the lake to your left, and when it pinches, just keep going south. I don't know how long exactly, but it's a big city. Can't miss it."

Luke turns the plane to the right. He drops altitude in the turn and over-revs the engines in response.

"You, uh, do a lot of flying?" the Firefighter asks when Luke levels back out.

Luke nods. "Some. Probably not enough. First take off by myself."

"Oh. Well, okay then. Congratulations?"

Luke holds the yoke in one hand and turns the GPS on with the other. He types in Minneapolis.

"Do you, uh, know how to land?" the Firefighter asks after a nervous pause.

"Not on land, no."

The Firefighter considers this. "I'm sure we have plenty of time to figure it out."

"Aviate, communicate, navigate. I skipped communicate," Luke reminds himself. He turns on the radio and listens to static. He slowly taps the scan dial, but it is apparent he doesn't know how to work the system. Out of options, he clicks the preset buttons and talks to each one.

"Any station on this net, any station on this net, medical emergency, need help."

He waits for a moment but hears nothing, so he flips to the next preset.

"Any station on this net, any station on this net, medical emergency, need help."

Nothing.

He continues this process, checking gauges and watching the horizon, while doing his best not to look behind him.

* * *

In the depths of a concrete building fifty miles south of Luke, the air traffic control at the 148th Minnesota Air National Guard hears a garbled transmission.

The Airman leans forward and keys his microphone. "Last calling, broken and unreadable. State your intentions. What is your call sign?"

In the sky, Luke hears and responds. "I'm in a Grumman Goose, my girlfriend has a traumatic injury to her head, and I need to get to Minneapolis." Luke tries to adjust the volume. "I'm going southeast along the lake. Lake Superior. Altitude… altitude is two thousand," he adds.

The Airman in the 148th Air Tower doesn't receive the message clearly because Luke has inadvertently changed the transmit channel on his radio instead of the volume. Luke's receive channel is locked, but his outgoing transmission channel is now mis-set. He also doesn't know that the 148th is one of a handful of full-duty air stations due to their proximity to the Canadian border, and they regularly participate in NORAD defense drills and air shows. Moreover, Luke will violate their airspace in just a few minutes.

The Airman at the air tower checks the radar and becomes concerned. "Unidentified aircraft heading south-southwest, reroute to airfield two-seven and land. Give call sign."

Luke turns to the Firefighter. "They won't talk to me without my call sign. What do I tell them?"

"Your nickname?"

Luke nods and keys the microphone. "This is... Spartan Goose."

The Airman at the 148th still hears none of this, so he hits an emergency button to alert the staff of a possible real-world response.

The shift manager hurriedly enters. "What is it?"

"This plane," the Airman starts, pointing at the radar. "No transponder, last transmission claimed a medical emergency on board but is no longer communicating."

"Where'd it come from?"

"Just popped up, flying low, may have come out of Canada."

The manager takes a microphone and speaks into it. "This is not a drill. This is not a drill."

Outside, two pilots run to their F-16s, and the Duluth airport is temporarily closed. The jets take off on full afterburner, which in the early morning could be seen by anyone awake and heard by all those still sleeping. The pilots receive their brief in-flight and rapidly close the distance. They are traveling at over a thousand miles an hour to the Goose's one-seventy-five.

Luke never sees them coming, and when they pass by him at no less than a few hundred feet, he is absolutely startled.

"What was that?" he shouts.

The F-16s bank hard. One comes behind the Goose while the other pulls up to his left side.

"Unidentified aircraft, this is Viper 1-1. Identify your intent," the one next to him says.

Luke can hear this and waves at the pilot. "I'm Spartan Goose!"

Viper 1-1 sees Luke talking but not transmitting. He communicates this to his wingman on a secure channel.

"Viper 1-2, the pilot is talking but not transmitting."

Viper 1-1 then addresses the Goose directly. "Give me a thumbs up if you can hear me."

Luke gives Viper 1-1 a thumbs up.

Viper 1-1 nods. "All right, turn on your transponder and land at Duluth. We will escort you."

Luke presents a thumbs down, shakes his head, and points further forward.

The pilot is annoyed but doesn't get the impression that Luke is a threat. "Viper 1-2, pilot is indicating he won't land, and instead wants to keep going. Hold while I figure out what's going on." He then switches over to Luke. "I need you to communicate. Confirming you can hear me, right?"

Luke gives him a thumbs up, then taps his headphones and raises his hands indicating he doesn't know why it isn't working.

Viper 1-1 works with this. "All right, follow your headphone cable and make sure that it's plugged all the way in."

Thumbs up from Luke.

"All right, check that your transmission channel is on the same channel as the receive since it is working just fine. Whatever you do, don't change your receive channel."

Luke looks at the radio and sees the transmission dial is turned to a different setting than the receiving one. He adjusts it, and Viper 1-1 hears Luke for the first time.

"How's this?"

"Good. Now state your intent."

"Call sign Spartan Goose. I need to get to Minneapolis. My girlfriend got hit in the head at a house fire in Silver Bay, and she needs a trauma hospital."

"All right, land at the airfield, and we will transfer your patient to an ambulance."

Luke looks back at Stella. She takes very shallow breaths. "Negative, no can do. Need to get to Minneapolis, time now."

The Air Traffic Controller comes in on another frequency.

"Viper 1-1, Silver Bay fire department confirms a house fire, medical emergency, and one Grumman Goose taking off with a very adamant junior pilot and one very injured patient. We're switching from incursion protocol to escort. How copy?"

"Aye-firm, home base. Viper 1-1 and 1-2 escorting."

Luke doesn't hear any of this, and Viper 1-1 keys back in on Luke's channel. "Spartan Goose. What's your status?"

"I'm fine. Stella's not."

"Roger, and the plane?"

Luke looks at dials and readings. He inadvertently jostles the yoke a bit too much, and the large Goose moves dramatically to the left. Viper 1-1 lifts away before Luke can get any closer. Luke doesn't register this as he is focused on the instruments and finishing the assessment.

"Fuel is full, I'm not redlining anything, and nothing is doing anything it shouldn't. That's good, right?" he asks as he steadies the plane and looks back at Viper 1-1.

Viper 1-1 has come back into position and nods. "Yeah, that's good. You're twenty minutes out from Minneapolis. Is your intent to land at the airport downtown?"

Luke takes a moment to appreciate the situation. "Never been there, but if that's what it takes to get her to a neurosurgeon, then yes, that's my intent."

"Copy all, Spartan Goose. Give me a minute while I relay so they can coordinate with airport EMS."

"Thank you."

Viper 1-1 changes channels and talks to home base, and Viper 1-2 moves from the rear of the plane to the right side. She inspects the Grumman, and a large gash of metal catches her eye. She closes in for a better look and is concerned with what she sees.

"Viper 1-1, Viper 1-2," she radios.

"Go for 1-1."

"Starboard-side landing gear looks destroyed."

Viper 1-1 considers this. "Spartan Goose, Viper 1-1 here. If you look to your right, Viper 1-2 is saying your right-side landing gear might be inoperable. Did you hit anything?"

"Dammit," Luke breathes. "Yeah, the dock."

"Want to try lowering your gear for me? Might need to slow down for a little bit, but better we know now than later."

Luke feathers the throttles back and watches the airspeed indicator slide to just over a hundred knots. "All right, I've slowed down. How do I lower landing gear? I've never landed on land before."

Viper is concerned. "Oh? How, uh, how much flying have you done?"

"A few takeoffs, some water landings. Maybe ten hours total."

"Well then, that changes things a little bit. Let's research the process for you. Hold on."

They call home base and dig out an old Grumman Goose manual. Luke is talked through the steps, but only the left gear extends.

"Viper 1-2, anything good?"

Viper 1-2 shakes her head. "Negative, no movement. Leaking hydraulics."

Viper 1-1 responds. "Roger, Spartan Goose, hold what you've got. We need to make a plan B."

Luke sighs and looks back. Stella is breathing quickly, but is still unconscious. The Firefighter is looking over her and takes her vitals.

"How's she doing?" Luke asks.

The Firefighter doesn't feel comfortable answering and asks a distracting question. "When do we land?"

"Soon, hopefully," Luke replies.

"You know, for never having flown, you're doing a great job."

Luke looks at the GPS and zooms into Minneapolis, then over to Saint Paul. He studies the map, and an idea crosses his mind. "Ever landed on water before?"

The Firefighter shakes his head. "No, why?"

Luke comes over the radio. "Viper 1-1, is there water near the hospital? I can land this right next to the building if need be."

"Spartan Goose… that's not the worst idea I've ever heard."

Home base, which has monitored the entire conversation, comes over the radio. "Pigs Eye Lake?"

Viper 1-1 is skeptical. "Needs more runway… the Mississippi runs right next to the airport."

"And turns right by the city," Viper 1-2 adds.

"Done," Luke commits. "Just guide me in."

"You sure?"

"Don't ask me again, I might change my mind."

Viper 1-1 nods. "Sounds like a plan."

There is a moment of silence as everyone processes the information. During that time, Luke finally finds a moment to worry.

"Is it a good hospital?" he asks the Vipers.

"Viper 1-2 here, yes. Both my kids were born there."

"Well," Luke says, looking over to his right, "that's as solid of a recommendation as I can ask for. I'll take it."

Viper 1-1 verbalizes the plan. "All right, we're going to come in from the east to keep the sun out of your eyes. Viper 1-2 will maintain your right-side wing, and I'll be in front and above you to maintain your approach. The rest is up to you."

An update from the Duluth Air Traffic Controller focuses their attention on what lies ahead. "Ambulances will be standing by for transport on both sides of the river depending on where you end up. Coast guard is clearing the waterways of boats and barges. Air traffic at St. Paul's has put everyone on racetracks. You guys'll be the only ones in the air… and the water. Good luck"

"Viper 1-1 copies all."

"Viper 1-2 copies."

There's a pause, and the Firefighter taps the back of Luke's seat.

"Spartan Goose copies," Luke responds.

"Spartan Goose, Viper 1-1, we're a few minutes out. You ready?"

Luke exhales a breath, "Ready."

Viper 1-1 nods. "Roger, I'm going to jump ahead and do a practice run. I want to make sure the landmarks are good and it's safe to commit."

The F-16 rips ahead of the Goose at the speed of sound. It flies away, and Luke sees the city of Minneapolis grow in front of him. Tall glass buildings, wide sprawl, and highways reveal their details, and the Mississippi River meanders by it. Off to the side and closer to him, St. Paul, with its slightly shorter buildings, becomes prominent.

Luke starts to take this all in and wonders if he's going to pull it off.

"Just hit the ball hard," he whispers.

From far below, several people on Highway 10 see Viper 1-1 fly low and fast. The plane approaches Pigs Eye Lake, roars along the river, then flies over the city. It is gone as fast as it has arrived, and people lose sight of it in the morning sun.

Viper 1-1 reassumes its position next to the Grumman a moment later. "Spartan Goose. Looks good. Follow us in."

"Following. And… if this doesn't pan out, thanks for trying."

"Any time."

Luke feels it appropriate to salute the Vipers and receives two salutes in return.

Down below, ambulances and police cars rush to line the sides of the river in various patterns of flashing lights. A coast guard boat has blocked the orange-brown Mississippi, and river tugboats have pushed their barges to the sides. The boat crews, having nothing else to do, shut off their engines, stand outside, and look up. On the other side of the river, the St. Paul airport EMS and firetrucks rush across the tarmac to get into position, and closer to the city on the northern river bend, local news vans rush to strategic overlooks. Some block sidewalks while others park in handicap spots. Others are turned away by police cars, which have closed traffic between the Lafayette Bridge and Indian Mounds Regional Park.

And then it is silent, and everyone turns their attention toward the rising sun.

The Goose's throaty rumble is heard first, then three shadows cut through the air and break under the glare.

"Go for broke," the Firefighter says quietly over Luke's shoulder.

Luke concentrates on what he's about to do and nods to himself.

"Going for broke," he replies.

The plane's steady growl fades as Luke throttles down, extends the flaps, and makes minor adjustments. The city is in front of him, and he is mere feet over the highway below. The river looms ever larger and is flanked by green trees, and he passes so close he might have been able to see individual leaves if he weren't so focused on landing.

Viper 1-1 and 1-2 lead Spartan Goose over Pigs Eye Lake, then rise and break away as planned. Luke flies over an industrial park and fuel containers, then over a thin cut of trees. And then, it is directly over the Mississippi. The plane seems to maintain the same altitude longer than necessary, as if reluctant to commit, but then it comes down to the brown water in a smooth drop. It skips and sprays whitewash nearly a hundred feet from its belly, and the pontoons contrast greatly against the mud-churned river. The windshield is also covered in mist, and despite being safely on the surface, the plane doesn't slow down—it passes barges and the airport at near-takeoff speed.

The plane throttles along, past container barges and flashing lights, and only slows when the river turns west near the city. The plane's large rudder shifts, and it drives under the Lafayette Bridge. The motors echo loudly, and the people, reporters, and first responders gathered on top of the bridge rush across to the other side. The plane comes out quickly, and only then does it slow down.

The Goose's tail rudder shifts aggressively once more, and the plane turns to face Lambert's landing, just between Robert Street and the Lafayette Bridge. One engine cuts out, and the other still spins just as Stella had taught Luke to do, but there is no floating dock to approach straight on. Luke assesses the flat-sided concrete side of the river, and unable to park straight on, he throttles up, pushes the rudder, and swings the plane to the left. The right-side pontoon rips off as it hits the concrete landing, and the first responders duck under the wing as it shears the air above them. The side of the plane thuds against the concrete dock, and he shuts down the second engine.

The propellers stop, and everyone rushes to the plane. A quick moment later, the side door to the Grumman opens, and Luke comes out of it. He shouts for the paramedics to come on board and helps get Stella offloaded. They carry her toward an awaiting ambulance, the flashing doors shut, the sirens pierce the morning air, and it rushes into the city. A police escort roars ahead of it, and every intersection is blocked by emergency vehicles to ensure the ambulance gets through unimpeded.

Luke watches the escort make its way into the city, and only then, when he knows he has nothing left to offer, does he allow himself time to collapse in a shameless wave of emotion.

* * *

The emergency department at the hospital is standing by, and the trauma team wheels Stella to an awaiting CT scanner. She is evaluated and prepped for surgery a few minutes later.

Luke arrives in an ambulance and walks into the emergency room. He is shirtless, has a half-started IV in his arm, and marches straight to the nurse's station as if he weren't a patient at all.

"Where's Stella?" he asks firmly. "Which bay?"

The charge nurse steps forward—she expected him to come in, but not like this. "She's going in for scans and surgery," she says directly. "We'll know shortly. But let's get you taken care of because you've got a few burns, and that cut on your head needs attention."

"Not till I know she's going to be okay."

"She's in the best hands there are, and there's nothing you or I can do for her right now, is there? So, let's do the best for you. She'd want that, right?"

Luke recognizes her attempt at persuasion but doesn't have the energy to fight. "Yes. Okay. But no pain meds. I want to be conscious."

And with that, he allows himself to be led down the hallway to another room.

Chapter 8

Pierce and Bee rush through the hospital hallway. Pierce goes straight to the front desk and is about to talk to the nurse when he sees Luke in an arm sling, sitting on a chair in the hallway. There are a few bandages on Luke's head, and he is dressed in a hospital gown.

"Luke!" Pierce shouts.

Luke turns to them, and Pierce and Bee gingerly embrace him.

"I'm sorry. I'm really, *really* sorry," Luke says softly, tears welling in his eyes.

"No, no, no, no. You did nothing wrong. Where's Stella?"

"This room. Recovering. They won't let me in."

Bee wipes tears away. "The Cohls called us. We got here as quick as we could."

"I wish I had gotten here faster," Luke says somberly.

Pierce shakes his head and wipes his own tears away. "Maybe if you had landed on the hospital," he laughs. "Holy hell, how did you pull off a landing like that?"

Luke looks back at the room. "Stella taught me."

Bee holds his wrist. "What do they know about her?"

"They got her out of surgery an hour ago. She had a big brain bleed. Said if it had been any longer, it wouldn't have been good."

A Doctor comes out of Stella's room.

"Can we see her?" Pierce asks.

"Are you Stella's parents?"

"Yes, Bee and me, Pierce, and this is Luke."

The Doctor nods. "We had to remove a portion of her skull, here, to relieve the pressure. She'll be in a drug-induced coma for a few days until the swelling goes down, but I think chances are good for a full recovery, thanks to some amazing luck and flying skills."

Luke, Pierce, and Bee embrace each other and smile in a mixture of extreme relief and exhaustion.

* * *

A few days later, Stella lies in an ICU bed. The window blinds are open, and the sun is bright. Luke is in a button-down shirt, his arm in a sling, and the stitches on his head are cleaned up and covered. Bee and Pierce are there as well, and more than several get-well cards and flowers surround the room. A TV on the wall repeatedly plays the Grumman's miraculous river landing.

An Anesthetist closes off Stella's IV drip. "She's off the meds. Should start waking up soon."

Bee and Pierce hold Stella's hands while Luke paces. In a few minutes, Stella's eyes begin to open. She groans and moves a hand to her head.

Bee is the first to speak. "Stella, can you hear me? Can you see us?" she asks.

Stella nods gingerly. "Hmm… Mom. What happened?"

Pierce cries, "Oh, sweetheart, what didn't happen?"

Stella sees Luke and reaches out to him, "What are you doing here?"

Luke grins and comes to her side. "You know, just hanging out."

"What happened to your arm?" she asks, squinting.

"Hurt it a little bit. Nothing serious."

Stella looks around and sees the TV in the corner. She recognizes her father's airplane and looks at it quizzically. "Dad… why's the Goose in the river?"

"Oh, honey, there's a lot to catch up on," Pierce chuckles as he wipes tears away.

Stella keeps watching the news feed, which now shows Luke throwing the plane's door open and ushering the EMS crew in.

She turns her head to Luke. "You flew?"

"And landed!" Pierce exclaims.

"Why?"

"You got your head bumped," Luke says gently.

Stella touches the bandages on her head, then tries to sit up. She grimaces in pain and lies back down.

"What happened?" she asks.

"House fire," Luke says. "Do you remember any of it?"

Stella thinks a moment and recollects. "Yeah… did everyone get out?"

Luke and her parents exchange a somber look.

"What? What is it?" she asks.

Bee tries to reassure her "The Cohls are fine. And Luke saved the last kid. House was a total loss, but…"

"But?"

"Stella, honey," Pierce starts, "Saint…"

Stella grows stern. "Where is he?"

"He's gone," Luke says, feeling a strong sense of responsibility since he was the last person to see him. "The house burned for almost a whole day, and the fire was so intense they couldn't even find his…"

"Oh, Saint," Stella says quietly.

"But he saved one of the kids," Luke says with a proud smile. "And he fought the fire to the very end. And… he told me it was okay to go. So, I went."

There's a knock on the door. The Station Chief from the Silver Bay fire department is led in by a Nurse. He is dressed smartly in his class As and carries flowers. He has been inundated with interviews and investigations all week since the story made national news.

"Chief, how are you?" Luke asks, having spoken with him earlier.

"I'm dropping these off," he says, handing the flowers to Bee and turning to Stella. "I heard you might be coming out today. Glad to see you're doing well."

There is a moment of appreciation, and he turns to Luke afterward, "Also, Luke, I was wondering if I could ask you something. In private?"

Luke turns to Stella.

"Go, I'm fine," she says.

"Okay, I'll be right outside," Luke reassures.

He steps out into the hallway with the Chief. "What's up?"

"She looks like she's going to be okay."

Luke nods, "Yes, she remembers the fire. That's a good sign."

"That fire spread faster than anything I've ever seen," the Chief continues. "Probably a nest in the chimney. But there's something else I wanted to ask," he clarifies.

"Sure, what is it?"

"Uh, in your report, you said you flew down with a firefighter?"

Luke nods, "Yeah, he was with me the whole time. Don't know where he went after I landed, but there was so much going on. I want to make sure he gets the credit he deserves."

The Chief looks around, then back at Luke, concerned. "Son, there's nobody in my department by that description, and none of them flew in the plane with you. They were all fighting the fire."

"What?"

The Chief knows that smoke inhalation and shock can yield all sorts of responses, so he tries to take it easy with the facts. He places a hand on Luke's shoulder and talks softly, "I'm saying that it was just you and Stella on that plane. No one else."

Luke pauses and tries to take this in as a chill runs down his back. "But he was with me… I felt him."

* * *

A week later, Stella sits in a wheelchair, and Luke pushes her down a hospital hall. Her head is bandaged up, and his arm is in a sling, but the fresh fall day is spectacular, and they have convinced the doctors to let them take lunch in the park across the street.

"So," the Nurse clarifies before letting them out of her sight. "No flying, no race car driving, and be back in a few hours. I mean it," she says with playful seriousness.

They laugh in agreement and Luke takes Stella to the park. The leaves are in a final brilliant display of reds, yellows, and oranges. They shuffle along the sidewalk and marvel at the explosion of color.

Luke is midstory as they cross through the center of the park. "And then the F-16s, they flew so close, like, from me to that car. And the pilots walked me through everything. It was amazing."

Stella beams at Luke as he speaks, and they approach a hotdog vendor. She points it out.

"Hungry?"

"Very."

Luke orders two dogs, she asks him to put spicy mustard on hers, and they each take a bite and relish it.

"And then?" she asks.

"And then what?"

"Now that you know how to fly, are you going to get a pilot's license?"

Luke laughs and flaps his slung elbow. "I probably need a copilot. You know anyone recently out of work and not cleared to fly until doctors say their skull has healed?"

Stella giggles. "I just might."

Luke leans down and kisses her. "Good."

His phone rings, and he doesn't immediately pick it up, but Stella nods and indicates he should take it. He checks the number and doesn't recognize it.

"Hello?"

"Hey, is this the guy from Montana?" the person on the other line asks.

"It might be," Luke says, sensing familiarity.

"Missing your dog again?"

Luke remembers the Gruff Voice to be that of the microchip phone number. He indicates to Stella that everything is okay and takes a few steps away from her.

"I am. Well, uh, we lost him in a fire," Luke says solemnly.

Gruff Voice considers this. "Hmm, well that's interesting. I just got a call from a Firefighter, saying he wanted you to know that he and the dog are doing just fine."

"What?"

Gruff Voice clears his throat. "Yeah, all he said was that he's proud of you, and he and the dog are doing just great—and that I needed to relay the message. Didn't get a name or nothing, and the number didn't show up. Sorry about that."

Luke looks over at Stella. She licks mustard off a finger and notices him watching her. She smiles and winks, and he smiles back before returning his attention to the phone call.

"That might be the best news I've heard all day. Thank you," Luke says quietly.

Gruff Voice considers this. "I guess the dog won't be running off anymore?"

Luke smiles and looks around. A few leaves flutter to the ground, a pair of robins fly to a tree, and he remembers Emily's words.

We don't always have to understand the gift. Sometimes we are just meant to accept it.

Luke takes a deep breath and allows himself to feel deeply settled. "He's home now. So, no, I don't think he will be."

"Well, it sure has been an adventure," Gruff Voice says with a hint of closure.

"It definitely has been. Have a great day, and thanks for letting me know."

They hang up, and Luke stands a moment longer. He looks down at his phone, then puts it away. He looks over at Stella, and she reaches for him to come closer.

"Everything okay?" she asks.

Luke recognizes her to be more beautiful than ever. He takes her hand and kisses it, then her forehead, then her lips.

"If you only knew."

She grins. "After all we've been through? Try me."

THE END

www.ingramcontent.com/pod-product-compliance
Lightning Source LLC
Chambersburg PA
CBHW031530310726
48971CB00008B/2424